Praise for Deni

"Denis Bell's collection of short fiction *A Box of Dreams, 2nd edition,* centers itself in the tradition of *Spoon River Anthology* (minus the tombstones) and *Winesburg, Ohio. A Box of Dreams* is dark without a trace of cynicism: it invites empathy for even the least attractive of the characters; these protagonists commonly suffer from mangled memories, rightful guilt, and an inability to distinguish between delusion and reality, between past and present. The stories tease and tantalize: truth glimmers between the lines. Louise Freshman Brown's gorgeous images are haunting illuminations."

-Miriam N. Kotzin, author, *Country Music,* Spuyten Duyvil Press

"Denis Bell and flash fiction represent a marriage made in Heaven. The two dozen short works in his collection, A Box of Dreams, show him working at the top of his game. In each, the reader's mind is taken for a weird, wonderful walk that's by turns wryly humorous and darkly intriguing. Louise Brown's illustrations lend just the right atmosphere for an absorbing read."

- Paul Blaney, Writer in Residence, Rutgers University,
author, *The Anchoress*

"Each piece in Denis Bell's *A Box of Dreams* is a work of magic that moves steadily along, pulling you in, and not letting you go… The stories are by turns haunting, heartbreaking and funny, and they never fail to surprise… Blending the real with the surreal, these stories, more than anything else, get to the heart of our humanity, our vulnerabilities, and they do so in a way that represents the best in flash fiction."

-Dennis Pahl, Long Island University, Editor for *Confrontation Magazine*

A Box of Dreams

Stories by Denis Bell,

Illustrations by Louise Freshman Brown

LUCHADOR PRESS

Luchador Press

Big Tuna, TX

First edition 1 3 5 7 9 10 8 6 4 2

ISBN: 978-1-952411-11-3

LCCN: 2020946909

Author photos: Denis Bell

Artwork: Louise Freshman Brown

Acknowledgements

I want to thank the people who, in one way or another, made this book possible. Louise for her great art work. Writers like Nancy Stohlman and Bob Thurber, whose words first made me aware of the power of flash fiction. Howard and Ruth Bell, for their encouragement and their numerous insightful suggestions regarding my stories. The editors of the literary magazines who accepted the stories for their journals (and some who rejected them). Justin and Madison, for starting me off on the literary road. Most of all, Cindy, for her everlasting love and support.

Denis Bell

I wish to thank Denis for asking me to illustrate "A Box of Dreams, a collection of short stories." His insight into the connection between his stories and my imagery resulted in a collaboration that resonated with rhythmic intuitive responses. It became a unique visual/verbal confluence of creativity.

Louise Freshman Brown

Contents

Dedicated to the memory of Phyllis and Philip Bell

A Box of Dreams

Time Lapse

My name is Arthur Pinte and I teach Philosophy at a Liberal Arts College in South Carolina. One day my teenage daughter shows me a collection of short stories that she and her friends have been reading, titled *The Machine of Time.*

The book is something of a sensation—the flavor of the season—having forged its way to the top of the best-seller lists and in the process beating out the memoirs of a well-known political blowhard. The volume is a collection of short stories, all by different authors, written on the common theme of time travel. The title is no doubt a nod to H G Wells' famous work. My daughter keeps telling me that I must read it and eventually I do.

The book is most enjoyable. The stories are of varying quality, some excellent, some not so great. I think that maybe I can write something as good as some of them myself.

So, one Friday afternoon, after I've finished grading the weekly batch of dreary online essays, I decide to give it a shot. Being of a philosophical bent and always having been intrigued by the idea of time travel—the grandfather paradox and all that, I think I can put together something halfway decent.

A few days later, there it is! "Time Lapse." My first literary work. Not Kafka or Joyce, to be sure, but not bad nonetheless. If I do say so myself.

I ought to point out that I have no plans to publish the story at his time. I only wrote it for my own amusement and it has served its purpose well in that regard. My wife is not quite so amused, the poor woman having been subjected to a thousand revisions of the story, each more trivial than the last, but that's another matter.

On a whim, I email the story to one of my professional colleagues, a well-known figure in the world of Philosophy, who happens also to be a published Science Fiction writer. He reads the story, likes it, and, somewhat to my surprise, suggests that I try to publish it.

I think, why not? Nothing ventured, nothing gained.

I send the story to a slew of literary magazines: sci-fi, fantasy, mystery, Gothic, mainstream, serious, wacky. Some famous, some obscure, some highly renowned, some not, even a couple of gay ones.

And they all reject it, one after the other.

The rejection letters run the gamut of political correctness and tact:

"Dear Arthur, thank you for submitting 'Time Lapse' to *Stranger Than Life* but it does not meet our needs at the present time."

"Dear Mr. Pinte, unfortunately 'Time Lapse' is not a fit for *Breadbox*. We thank you for thinking of us and wish you the best of luck in placing this story elsewhere."

"Dear Author, we have read with interest your short piece. We regret that…"

Now, I'm not exactly devastated by the news. Firstly, as you recall, I hadn't intended to publish the thing in the first place. Secondly, I am well aware that writers of all stripes face rejection at some stage of their career, the *über*-example perhaps being Stephen King, one of the most commercially successful writers of all time, who, by his own account, papered his entire kitchen with little pink rejection slips before receiving a contract for his first novel. Thirdly, I already have a somewhat satisfying, if unspectacular, career as an academic and I'm not about to give up my day job any time soon. In fact, having published several articles in my discipline, I'm hardly a stranger to the pink slip. The "R" in my middle name actually stands for Rejection, though some people think it's Raymond.

I dust myself off, go on with my life, and write a few more stories.

A few months later, I'm reading over "Time Lapse" for the umpteenth time, but the first time in a while, and I come to a revelation. It actually kind of sucks! If I were an editor, I wouldn't want to publish something like that either. *What on earth was I thinking?*

So I sit down and I revamp the story. We're talking major overhaul here, not minor tune-up. I rewrite the stilted dialogue, show rather than tell, turn the static into the dynamic, add immediacy, vibrancy, and verve. Of course, I thought I'd done all that the first time around. Whatever, it's better now. Still not Kafka or Joyce, but what you gonna do?

I would like to publish this new version of the story, but I'm faced with a dilemma. I sent the first version to all the journals under the sun and they all rejected it. I don't want to send the new version back to the same places.

So I scan through my database of literary magazines and eventually I come across one that I had not noticed before. An obscure little rag called *The McMuffin*, published out of a community college somewhere in the Midwest. Not oriented towards sci-fi but I think, what the hell, shouldn't be too hard to publish in something like *that*, right?

I send "Time Lapse" on steroids there.

A couple of days later, I open my Inbox and there is an email from The McMuffin.

Now, in my short and unsuccessful writing career, I've received a few of these quick responses from journals. Usually they are form acknowledgements, "Dear so and so, we look forward to rejecting your work." (They actually say "reading" of course, but I've become a little jaded.) Sometimes they inform that the journal is currently closed to fiction and please resubmit at such and such later date. One was a notification that the journal is closing its pages. So as you might imagine, I open the email without a huge amount of enthusiasm. It reads as follows.

Dear Arthur Pinte,

Thank you for submitting "Time Lapse" to *The McMuffin*. Although we are unable to publish your work at this time, we thank you for the opportunity to review it. *The McMuffin* is a journal that lives beyond the edge, and seeks to explore the boundaries, of existence. Our editorial policy reflects our unique character and our timeless nature. We have a rigorous review process. We read every manuscript with the utmost care and extend to each one the precise degree of attention that we feel it deserves. The process can be quite lengthy. This accounts for our inordinately long delay in responding to your submission. Please be assured that our tardiness in this matter is a direct reflection of the respect that we accord to those who are so kind as to grace us with their words.

Sincerely,

Peter Spires, Chief Editor

Seeks to explore the boundaries of existence. Their *unique character and timeless nature. Those who are so kind as to grace us with their words.* Pretentious claptrap and silly overblown rhetoric.

And the McMuffin has evidently found a new angle on tactful: "Extend the precise degree of attention that we feel it deserves... inordinately long delay... our tardiness is a direct reflection of the respect..." They have the nerve to send this out after *two days*!

I delete the email and vow to forget about it and The McMuffin.

But I don't. I *can't.* As I've said, I'm used to this story being rejected but this business is more than a little irksome. Are they perchance extracting the Michael? Siphoning the urine? Poking fun at li'l ole me?

I stew on the matter for a couple of days, then figure out an appropriate response. A response of a *literary* nature, if you will. I will prepare a thinly veiled memoir piece satirizing the treatment that the words with which I graced *The McMuffin* received, and send it there as a new submission. I don't expect them to publish it of course, but I will have the last laugh.

I knock the story off in an hour or so. Heck, the thing more or less writes itself. A triumph of irony and pique containing several snide little put downs of The McMuffin and its timeless editorial policy. The editor will be mortified.

I'm sitting in front of my tablet getting ready to send it. It's the new type that they recently introduced, where you think your commands at the machine. I'm still trying to get the hang of it. Eventually, I manage to navigate to my Deleted folder and locate the relevant item.

From	Subject	Date Sent	Size
The McMuffin	Time Lapse	10/1/2010	0 KB

I think REPLY several times and nothing happens. As I'm reaching for the screen, cussing out this piece of "alpha-synchronized" wizardry that set me back a cool two grand, I happen to notice the date on the email. *October 1, 2010.* Twenty years ago! And the size of the file— *zero K?*

I check the dates and the sizes of some of the other items in the folder. They all seem about right. I read the letter over. The language, which struck me as pretentious before, now seems downright weird. A journal that *lives beyond the edge of existence?*

I decide to check out the journal's website www.mcmuffin.org and find that the link doesn't work. (Try it—you'll see.)

Finally, I Google "The McMuffin." There are a huge number of hits, but almost all of them refer to the breakfast sandwich. Eventually, I come to a small Wikipedia entry for the magazine.

> **The McMuffin** was an American literary journal published between 2005 and 2011. The journal was founded by Peter Spires, a professor of English at Burkett Community College in Grand Rapids, Michigan. The journal became defunct

> after Spires was killed in a car crash in September of 2010.

The dead evidently have no sense of time!

I reopen my database and scroll down to the appropriate section.

Alternate Dimensions

Bête Noir

Bizarre Tales

…

The Assistant

He didn't need an assistant, but they sent him one anyway. One morning he looked up and there she was. A tightly wrapped woman, all bustle and business. She quickly established herself at the spare desk in the corner of his office.

The woman looked familiar. He studied her as she worked at the desk, trying to figure out when and where they might have met before. Perhaps she reminded him of an actress he'd seen in a movie or a writer on the cover of one of the mystery novels he devoured so hungrily? Nothing quite seemed to fit.

Eventually, he decided she looked like a girl he'd known in college and resolved to forget about the matter.

The Assistant proved to be... unpredictable. Every now and then she would turn her head and stare at him, smiling a slow sad smile, as though somehow privy to his inner world. He hated the disappointment he saw in those eyes and pretended not to notice it. The next day, his coffee girl—all sweetness and light!

By turns shy, bold, severe, sassy, playful, demure, forward, aloof… round and round they went. Nobody could be that flighty.

Perhaps this was her way of coming on to him?

He'd been alone so long the idea was stimulating. He thought about it as he lay in his bed at night, concocted midnight scenarios.

By day, he wondered about her. How she had shown up so unexpectedly. How he had taken her in so readily. Perhaps she has a hidden agenda, he thought jokingly. *Corporate spy.*

He made a series of discreet inquiries and came up empty. She was unlisted in the company directory. When he asked one of his colleagues if she knew anything about her, the woman looked uncomfortable and turned away.

He played a little game with himself where he pretended that the Assistant existed only in his mind. *A nice irony*, he thought, the sort of thing you read about in short stories of the more pretentious kind.

Eventually, he decided he was going to have to get to the bottom of this matter. Attempt to determine her position in the company hierarchy, the nature of the strange tension that existed between them.

The only viable approach seemed to be the direct one, though it ran contrary to his nature. He would talk to her, explain how he'd come to feel about her in the however long they had worked together, that he wanted to take their relationship to the next level.

He'd do it this week, tomorrow perhaps, if the opportunity presented itself.

He rehearsed the speech, over and over: *We've known each other now for...* It sounded so lame compared with the thunder clouds gathering in his head.

A doctor's appointment the next day kept him out of the office until noon. By the time he arrived, she was gone. He assumed that she was out sick and waited for a call, but the hours ticked by and none came.

Then he noticed the unusually tidy desk. Found the beginnings of a note crumpled up in the wastebasket. No reason. No forwarding address. *Nothing.* He beat his head against the wall in an agony of rage.

He searched for her all over town. In supermarkets, bookstores, coffee shops and bars. Posted ads in personal columns, conducted online searches. Tacked flyers up in public places using a likeness of her that he sketched:

HAVE YOU SEEN THIS WOMAN?

Even offered a reward, as though she were an outlaw or a lost puppy.

A few dead ends, then zilch. He felt like a man drowning in his own juices.

He beat his head some more.

Not too much of that now, she says as he reaches for the salt.

Just like a wife, he mutters, and she giggles. Musical laughter, like the tinkling of broken glass. Later, they'll play *Scrabble* together in the lounge—perhaps she'll let him win for a change. The others will no doubt stare at them and shake their heads and smirk, but what do they know?

She's with him all the time now, his Assistant. Beside him watching TV. Waiting for him when he returns to his room at night. Nestled against him in bed when he wakes up in the morning. Forever young, like Bart Simpson, or a dead classmate, or a song on Prom night. *Devil with a Blue Dress.*

Delivery

“It came out positive.”

"You're kidding!”

It would seem so. The news was surprising to Ruth because Sandra was old. Not Betty White old, but easily old enough to be Ruth’s mom.

“What did Jim say?”

“I didn’t tell him.”

“Sandy, he’s gonna have to know sometime.”

Sandra didn’t even bother to reply to this, just twisted her mouth into the expression of disgust that she assumed at times.

“You ought to see a doctor, sometimes those tests are wrong. There was this one chick I knew in high sch–”

"It's not wrong, I checked it out. When they say no sometimes it’s yes, but when they say yes it’s always yes.”

Sandra looked down at her stomach, as though she expected to see it expanding. Not yet, after two months. Anyway, she’d always been kind of chubby. She would be chubbier still. Like a balloon. She knew the changes her body would go through, she'd done it once before. A long time ago, but she knew. Vomiting. Bloating. Back pain towards the end. The sheer strangeness of something growing inside her, a part of her and yet… *not.* Women were supposed to like it. Did this mean she was not a real woman?

“Perhaps he’ll be happy about it. My sister's boyfriend was when she told him she was pregnant with my niece."

Yes, thought Sandra, though this was something else she assumed he had given up on long ago. Laying around the house all day in his underwear, drinking and farting and picking at the sores on his legs. Yelling obscenities at the TV and passed out on the couch by 8:00 pm. That which he claimed to want most in the whole world, their failure in this regard brought out as a club against her time and again, she had the power to give it to him now.

She had the power.

The thought was so strange, it seemed to lack meaning.

Meanwhile, Ruth was carrying on nine to the dozen about the sister and it seemed necessary to contribute something to the conversation.

"So, are they?"

"Huh?"

"Happy?"

"She thought so for a while. Then one day he just up and left. Told her he needed his freedom."

Freedom. This word had so many meanings. Sandra had lived with several men in her time and they always seemed to come up with some or other version of it when things went south.

"He doesn't want it, he only thinks he does. He hasn't worked in three years."

Sandra was becoming a little distraught.

"*How can we…*"

Ruth reached out an arm and drew Sandra towards her.

"Don't worry sweetie, it will be alright. You'll manage, people always do."

Spoken with the deep wisdom of twenty-four years of life, thought Sandra.

There had been a delivery of muffler parts earlier in the day. Sandra picked up a box and started towards the back of the store with it.

"You shouldn't be doing that! Call Pete."

Pete was busy with a customer. Sandra would carry the box herself, and the other boxes too. Tonight, she would be the one doing the drinking in the Krogh household. The booze would help some but it too would not put an end to this nightmare. One day next week she would call in sick and visit a doctor. But not the kind that Ruth was thinking of and she wouldn't ever tell Jim about it.

Friends

We're all together now. I'm the second one from the left. The one with the pretty mouth and the long lustrous hair but it's hard to tell because I hide myself in this place. The one with the big head and the holes for eyes is *Larry*. The eyes are usually directed at me but today they have found a different target. Larry was one mean son of a bitch but he sure knew how to love. I did too back then, perhaps a bit too much. Then there is *Carl*. Carl told me once that he knew Larry. Knew him like last week's leftovers he said but with Carl you could never be sure because Carl was crazy. Carl was in the construction business. Destruction too, as it turned out. Threatened me once with a hammer then had told me he would cut off his hands with his circular saw if I didn't take him back. Perhaps it was something else that needed cutting off? By that point I couldn't care. The one on the right is *Bert*. The dapper one with the moose breath and the club foot. Bert the Flirt, the young women at the nursing home used to tease him and he liked it, the old fool. In some ways Bert was the best of the whole bunch. Or the worst. I never could quite decide and I was with him twenty years. At least Bert told me that he loved me. But then Bert loved everybody and Bert could love and hate at the same time. Larry, Carl and Bert. I loved them all in my day. And I gave myself to them. At least, I think I did. It's hard to know now because all there is to go by is what I have left.

Einstein's Wardrobe

There is a story, most likely apocryphal, that is told about Einstein. That his entire wardrobe consisted of five identical suits. When asked about this, he is alleged to have said, "So I don't waste my brain in the mornings deciding which set of clothes to wear."

Einstein and I are similar in this respect, if in no other. I have five tee shirts of the same color, two others in a very similar shade and style, two pairs of blue jeans, thirteen—after the last wash—identical socks, and a single pair of shoes.

I am, or rather I *was*—it seems strange to use the past tense—a professor of English at a Liberal Arts college in South Carolina. Students frequently used to comment on my teaching evaluations, "He wears the same clothes to class every day." This wasn't true, of course—except as regards the shoes—it just *appeared* that way. Apparently, the students at Templeton didn't know the Einstein story.

I had managed to gain for myself a reputation for being absent minded, in a fashion more befitting a math professor than the litterateur that I am. To take just one example, one day I chose to walk to school rather than drive, the weather having been exceptionally mild that morning. Later in the day, I spent a good hour searching for my car in the parking lots before reporting it stolen to the Campus Police. Then they drove me home and there it was sitting bold as brass in the driveway! Within a couple of days everybody at the college had heard about the episode. But I digress, this is not the story that I want to tell.

The story that I want to tell began on a deceptively sunny, brutally cold day in January. I had just returned to my office after teaching Comparative Lit 526. A group of five students were clustered outside the door anxiously awaiting my arrival. This was rather unusual since office hours at Templeton—mine in particular—were generally not well attended, except for the period immediately prior to exams, and there were no quizzes or tests scheduled in any of my classes for another three weeks. I thought I had missed an appointment, but it proved not to be the case.

"Professor, we are wondering if your 2:30 class today is canceled."

'And why on earth would I do that?"

"You mean you haven't heard? It's all over campus. They're saying…"

At this point, the whole group started yammering and waving their arms and it was impossible to make out anything that was being said. It was like watching an episode of the McLaughlin Group. I rolled my eyes and raised a palm in the air.

"Suppose you all calm down, and *somebody* tell me what the hell is going on!"

It seemed that early that morning one of the cleaning crew had come across an open-topped box in Physical Plant A containing a white powder. Assuming the powder to be rat poison, but suspicious nonetheless, the cleaner passed the box on to her supervisor. The supervisor alerted the Campus Police, and they rushed it post haste to the authorities in town. Meanwhile, a small amount of the powder had found its way to the air intake that feeds a giant heat pump housed within the building. Physical Plant A provided heating and cooling to the east side of the campus, where the administrative offices were located. It turned out that classes at Templeton *were* canceled that day, and every day thereafter.

***

Templeton College was located in the sleepy little town of Cedar Hills, South Carolina. The school was founded around the end of the eighteenth century by a wealthy industrialist with the grandiose mission: "To provide outstanding young men with the type of robust education to prepare them to become leaders in society and in the world". Presumably there were no outstanding young women at that time, or if there were, then they were not expected to become either societal or world leaders.

The first students at Templeton were the sons of farmers, businessmen, artisans, teachers, and the like. The school became coed in the mid-sixties and rose in prominence. In recent years the student body has consisted largely of the children of doctors and lawyers and similar professional types. Soft, pasty-faced party kids with Porsches and trust funds, sharp in dress rather than intellect, with solid SAT's and old family connections, neither quite impressive enough to make it into the likes of Harvard or Princeton.

Geographically isolated, expensive, and lacking in serious academic distinction, Templeton was neither a hotbed of radicalism nor a bastion of conservative-ism, and it seemed strange that the school would be attacked in this fashion.

***

I arrived home around 2:30 that afternoon and immediately switched on the TV. All the local news channels were covering the story. By this time, the powder had been sent to a lab for analysis and, although it was clear to me that some key details of what would later come to be known as "The Templeton Incident" were being kept under wraps, the television coverage left no doubt that something very serious had happened in Cedar Hills that morning.

With FBI descending on the town like flies on a rotting carcass and experts from the CDC in Atlanta flying in, the town was buzzing like never before. The Police Commissioner had issued a statement earlier in the day calling for all persons in the vicinity of the college at the time of the incident to check themselves into Cedar Hills General for a series of medical tests.

I was not particularly concerned by this turn of events. I happen to be blessed with a singularly laid back, sunny disposition, and tend not to worry about things beyond my control.

I was, in fact, happy to have the afternoon off. I went to the local supermarket and bought a case of my favorite beer. I made a call from the pay phone opposite the store, then spent a couple of hours in the neighborhood bookstore reading excerpts from a new novel in the medical thriller genre that I enjoy. I called Sue, a girl I had been dating for the past couple of months, this time on my cell phone, and arranged to meet her for dinner.

We ate at Chan's. Needless to say, she had heard about the incident by that time and was beside herself.

"*Were you on campus when it happened?*"

"Of course I was on campus. You know I teach on Wednesdays."

"Well then, aren't you worried? I heard Dr. Sanjay Gupta on the six o'clock news talking about the stuff they found. It's some type of biological virus and they don't even know what this stuff does."

As opposed to a virus of the non-biological variety, no doubt.

"As it happens, no, I'm not. The buildings that were affected are on the east side of campus and the wind was from the west this morning. I'm perfectly okay. Hungry, too. I think I'll order the Emperor's Special."

"But you could be infected! Dr. Sanjay Gupta said— "

"Forget Dr. Sanjay fucking Gupta, will you. I told you, I'm perfectly fine! In fact, more than fine. Truth is, I'm feeling better tonight than I've felt for quite some time!"

She gave me a strange look, thinking perhaps that "the stuff" had found its way to my brain, and leaned back from the table.

"What say after the fortune cookies, we adjourn to my place and you and I do the nasty?"

"Are you *crazy*? You need to go get tested!"

The things we do for love! Of course, it had to be done anyway. I checked into CHG that night. The place was overflowing with forlorn looking inmates, the newly arrived medical experts, FBI agents, TV news crews, the works.

They were admitting, or more accurately, *confining*, everybody who was anywhere near the campus that day. We were assured we would be "made quite comfortable and would in all likelihood not have to stay longer than a few days." The phrase *in all likelihood* should have struck an ominous chord but nobody else there seemed to notice.

My first day inside the facility consisted of an interminable series of questions and questionnaires. Family history. Medical history. Buildings visited on the morning of the event. Present state of health. Chest pains? Shortness of breath? Bumps, welts, or swellings? On and on ad nauseam…

Then the probing and the scanning started up. Quite comfortable, my ass! No pun intended. Pricked and prodded, injected with radiographic chemicals and placed inside machines, tubes stuck into orifices, bodily substances of all manner extracted… Painful and disgusting though it all was, the worst torment was psychological rather than physical—the thought of being shut up with a bunch of about-to-be extreme sickies.

In any event, within a few days I was pronounced in the pink and allowed to leave. Many of my fellow inmates did not fare as well. It was later revealed that some of them never got out of there. But that's life—so to speak.

After the hospital, Sue and I continued to see each other for a couple of months, always at my apartment, as I seldom ventured outside any more. Since Templeton remained closed I no longer had teaching duties and that suited me just fine. I used the time wisely to finish an article on Poe and to conduct research for my forthcoming book on Dostoyevsky's *Crime and Punishment*. But that wasn't all I researched. From dawn to dusk I scoured the TV channels, radio stations and news sites looking for new developments in the case. Call it morbid curiosity if you are so inclined.

The weeks rolled by. Presidents Day came and went. Nothing had happened by the end of February. It was looking as though the saga had played itself out. Then one Friday afternoon, I switched on the TV and there it was!

Several senior administrators at Templeton College in Cedar Hills, South Carolina were stricken today with an as yet undiagnosed respiratory illness. College President Adam Levine, Provost Kenneth Gilbert, and Assistant Dean Susanna Gomez, are in critical condition and have been airlifted to Charleston for medical treatment. Levine's wife told reporters that her husband was due to play golf later in the day with Gilbert but woke with a high fever and coughing up blood. He lapsed into unconsciousness while being transported to the emergency room. Authorities strongly suspect a link between these events and the biological agent found on the Templeton campus on January 18. A spokesman for the…

Within a week, all three of them were dead! Soon after, other cases were reported. The first wave of casualties consisted mainly of administrators but also, unfortunately, some faculty, students, and support staff.

Naturally, I stayed within the confines of my sealed apartment, studiously avoiding all contact with the outside world. Superman in his fortress of solitude.

The Templeton virus proved to be both deadly and, after the incubation period, highly contagious. The CDC identified the virus as a virulent new strain of Anthrax and declared that if it were allowed to escape into the general population, the United States could suffer the worst pandemic since the outbreak of Legionnaires' disease. Thereafter, the town of Cedar Hills was placed under a strict quarantine. Military checkpoints were set up restricting travel in and out of town to those deemed essential personnel—purveyors of vital goods and services, doctors and paramedics, the deliciously euphemistically named "disposal teams," etc.

According to recent news reports, most of the downtown stores and businesses are now closed and boarded up. The busses stopped running over a month ago and there are almost no cars on the roads.

The few restaurants and bars that remain open are empty and silent. The streets are given over to the stricken and the demented. A sense of doom has descended on Cedar Hills. The town, like the people, is dying.

I remained untouched throughout all the turmoil and devastation, ensconced in my rooms with my supplies and my work, and, of course, the TV and Internet. There was a huge amount of media coverage in the subsequent months and I followed of every last bit of it.

***

Earlier this week, I was awakened shortly after noon by the ringing of my house phone. I'd been up most of the night working on the book and woke dazed and disoriented, and it took me a little while to get to the phone.

"I thought you weren't going to answer. Are you alright? It's Nancy."

"Nancy?" I was very groggy.

"Nancy Bloom."

"Oh, right, not quite with it yet. Had a late night yesterday. What's up?"

"I'm afraid I've got some bad news. Bill's wife passed away last night."

She was talking about Bill Sutcliffe, the Chair of Language Arts. I'd learned via emails from a couple of colleagues that his wife had recently come down with the virus, so it wasn't exactly a huge surprise. Nothing I needed to be dragged out of bed for at 9:30 in the morning.

"God, no! That's awful!"

"I'm taking up a collection on behalf of the department. There is a memorial service set for tomorrow at First Baptist on Seventh Street at 2:00 pm. Will you be able to make it?"

When hell freezes over.

"Of course I'll come. And put me down for twenty bucks, will you?"

What really jerked my chain was what she said just before she hung up.

"Have you seen today's *Post?* Looks like we're all on the job market now."

I'd stopped taking the newspaper a while back in keeping with my policy of splendid isolation, but as it turned out there was an article on the Yahoo News front page.

> **Demise of a college**
>
> ` May 15, 11:15 am (ET)
>
> CEDAR HILLS, SC. (AP) - The Templeton campus has been officially declared a Disaster Area. The now completed inspection of the campus shows that the virus has worked its way into the ducts in many of the buildings and it is expected that it will prove extremely difficult to eradicate. Several of the buildings will require gutting and refurbishing and others will need to be demolished entirely. The College Board of Regents issued a statement earlier today indicating that there are no plans to reclaim the campus. It seems that, after almost two hundred years, Templeton College, one of the nation's most distinguished seats of learning, will cease to exist as an academic institution.

There isn't much more to tell. Cedar Hills, South Carolina, hitherto little more than a jumped-up college town in the middle of nowhere, a stopover for motorists on Interstate 20, has now made it onto the world stage. In death lies immortality. Both town and gown are destined for a place in history alongside the Titanic, the Hindenburg, the Chernobyl nuclear plant, and the World Trade Centers. And all because of 3.5 ounces of white powder!

As soon as the quarantine is lifted, I'll be moving on. I'm in the process of packing up my belongings—books and papers, folders of news clippings, lab equipment, collection of war memorabilia, weapons, etc.

As it happens, I had made plans to leave Cedar Hills a while back. The fact is, in January of this year, I was denied tenure at Templeton! Thrown out onto the academic scrapheap after eight years, like a rusty Oldsmobile! By a bunch of washed up old stiffs—in spirit and now in body, too, some of them—unfit to lace my intellectual boots. As the saying goes, what goes around comes around.

The Feds are conducting an intensive investigation into the origin of the Templeton Incident, but it seems that, thus far, they have failed to come up with anything. Anyhow, I'm not worried. Why would I be? No one will ever believe that a man with Einstein's wardrobe, somebody who loses his car in his own driveway, is capable of anything.

Birthday Party

A kitchen paved with marble tiles. Granite counters topped with a punch bowl and a large vegetable platter, an ice cream cake and a stack of paper plates.

In a room down the hall a home movie is playing. Joanne chasing butterflies on a summer afternoon. Collecting snowflakes in winter. Hanging paper bats at Halloween. The magic of a first kiss. Getting wasted with Tina and Alex in a Volkswagen van on a road trip to Monterey. Riding bareback with Mark at a cabin in Big Sur. *Slow down*, Joanne says, *you'll be there before I'm ready.*

Exchanging gifts at a friend's baby shower, a panda bear and a hand-knitted sweater with a matching pom-pom hat. The date is April 12, 1980. Elizabeth is expecting a boy at the end of May. Perhaps they'll date in high school.

He won't be able to handle her, Joanne says.

The baby left her three months too soon and twisted something inside along the way. A tiny little thing, perfect in all ways but one.

A spare bedroom set aside for surplus items. A Munchkin costume from an old school play, kept all these years for no good reason. Portraits of family pets, long passed. The sweater with the hat, and a stroller.

In a corner of the room sits a beautiful child with eyes that look like Mark's. Joanne reaches out trembling hands and picks up the child. Feels for a moment the pulse beating inside the small chest, a rush of warm breath on her face. Feels a whole world filled with promise and wonder.

Joanne dresses the child in the sweater and sets her down gently in the stroller.

Back in the kitchen, a chef in a lab coat is hard at work preparing a feast. Plates piled high with raw nerves. A pot of something soft and pink blistering on the stove.

Excited shrieks erupt outside. A B-52 is coming in for an emergency landing and My Little Pony is kicking up a storm. A cousin packs up the mood in a plastic box to be buried in the back yard at the end of the day.

Elsewhere, the party is about to begin. Jimi Hendrix and Amy Winehouse are setting up in the lounge and River Phoenix is getting ready to welcome the guests.

Moving On

Billy dragged himself out of bed and looked down at his right thigh. The place seemed a little better today, but still hurt like an SOB. He rewrapped the wound the way they showed him at the hospital, threw on some clothes, and limped out to the garage.

***

"Holy crap! What *happened*, man?"

Billy looked down at his glass, ashen faced.

"Christine," he croaked.

"Christine? What did she do?"

"She… *exploded* on me, Jimbo."

"Exploded!"

"Yeah. Lucky to get out of there alive."

"Sheesh! What set her off?"

"Damned if I know. Never even saw it coming. One minute everything is hunky dory and the next…"

"No red light, then."

"Been beating my brains out over that ever since it happened. Keep thinking it was something I did. Or didn't, and should have."

"*You?* No way, man! You always took real good care of her. Why, I said to Sandy just last week, never saw a man so attentive as old Bill."

"I so much want to believe that."

"What happened to her… after?"

Billy shrugged. "They came and took her away."

"And you haven't seen her since, I suppose?"

"Nope. Nor do I intend to. Not if I can help it."

"Sounds like a frigging nightmare."

"You have no idea."

"Well it's good to see you out and about. Must say, I admire your gumption. I know how attached you were to her, and all. It's been what, five years now?"

Billy sighed. "Coming up on seven."

Jim whistled. "Seven years! Never kept one no more than three myself."

They sat in companionable silence for a couple of minutes. Then Billy managed a wry grin.

"Ah well, perhaps it's for the best."

"Oh, how's that?"

"Well, she was starting to show her age. And the way I figure it, the kind of shape she's in now, no way she is she ever gonna be… rehabilitated. Can her and move on."

"Amen to that, bro'!"

Billy was feeling a whole lot better. Amazing what a sympathetic ear and a couple of pints will do for the soul. He downed the last of his beer in one large swig, belched loudly, and wiped his mouth with his sleeve.

"Whatever, she's history now. And life does have its way of compensating us for our losses. Wait till you catch a load of the sweet little piece Louis fixed me up with."

"Cool! When do I get to meet the new queen?"

"*Charlotte?* She's right outside as we speak. I asked the valet to pull her up to the front door.

The Acrobat

The last time Jerry ever saw her, she was sporting a tee shirt with the slogan LION TAMERS DO YOU RIGHT emblazoned on the front.

They were in a coffee shop on Tremont and she was sitting alone at the next table. Jerry had seen her a few times wandering the neighborhood, once in the supermarket, but they had never before spoken. Now she seemed in the mood. She told him her name was Celeste. Then she said, "So, tell me a little something about yourself."

Jerry grew up as an only child on Long Island. His father had been an attorney and his mother a social butterfly and he worked out of his home trading stocks and writing articles for a local Arts & Culture magazine.

"Born and raised on a farm in Iowa."

"A country boy."

Jerry nodded. "Youngest of five. All slept in one room. No indoor plumbing. Walked three miles to get to school."

"My goodness!"

"Things were a little rough in those parts, back in the day. No social services. Ma was a shut-in and Pa was a… an *alkie*. Liked to beat us with his belt. Only when he was drunk though. When he was sober he was worse. Till he had his stroke, that is. But you don't want to hear all that."

"What is it you do for a living?"

"Kind of a Jack of all trades. Arc welding, construction when I can get it. Summers I work on an oil rig off the coast of Alaska."

Now she was looking amused. "The rugged type!"

They sat in silence for a moment.

"And you?"

"Hang around in dives talking to strange men and take my life in the palms of my hands?"

She smiled at him and showed him her palms. They were large, and calloused. Hands that had seen a lot of mileage in their time.

"No, really."

"Give you three guesses. Here's a hint. These hands were my lifeline once."

Three guesses as to what she did. Somebody who carries their belongings on their back would have been his first.

"Goal tender on a woman's soccer team!"

"No, silly."

"Masseuse?"

"Not even close."

"I give up. What?"

"I worked for a circus."

Now Jerry was amused. "A circus?"

"Yup."

"As a lion tamer?"

Celeste colored slightly. "No, the lion tamer was somebody else."

"So, what did you do there? At the circus."

"I was an acrobat. High trapeze. It's a very specialized thing."

Jerry looked at her arms. Looked at her shoulders. Looked at her waist. If this was an acrobat then he was a welder on an oil rig.

"It was a long time ago! I was young then. Retired from the business early."

"Had enough of the high life?"

Celeste shook her head. "I loved it," she said softly. "Flying above the whole world. I felt like a goddess up there. And they all loved me for it, the fools.

"Oh? No offence, but I didn't realize you trapeze acts were such a big deal. I guess the kids…"

"Those with kids took them to see the elephants. The ones that came for the high-wire were different.

"Different how?"

"People like that need something to take their minds off the holes in their lives. Booze or porn or pain, just so long as it's not theirs. Snake man. Monkey boy. Crazy lady. Then they see us up there doing our stuff and they imagine… they imagine it was *them* up there doing it even though they know they could never do that in a million years, and it makes them feel good for a while. I guess I was that for them. Most popular gal in the whole darn Midwest. Never once used a net."

"Well, that *is* crazy."

"None of us did back then. Not the good ones. A matter of professional pride."

"So if you loved it so much, why did you quit?"

"One day I fell."

"Really? It's a miracle you weren't…"

"Let's just say I'm tougher than I look. Like Bruce Willis in that movie. Unbreakable me! Except that…"

"Yes?"

"Except that I never did it again after that."

Now she looked on the verge of tears and Jerry felt like a jerk.

Jerry had had enough of their little game. He took out his wallet and removed a twenty-dollar bill. "Listen, I'm sorry if I…"

She glared at him like he had slapped her, but she took the money and stuffed it into the pocket of her pants.

After he was gone, she dug around in her backpack for a bottle of pain pills and a pack of cigarettes. Then she closed her eyes and set to rocking on her stool. Back and forth, she went, back and forth. And they shouted and cheered once more for their darling Celeste.

Part Time Employment

Everything you do in life comes back to haunt you eventually. The little things and the big. Lies that you tell. People that you hurt.

His big thing was Deborah Hirsch. They were Seniors together at Bridgeport High, so long ago it seemed like another lifetime. They were in a few of the same classes, but they never spoke. He would see her in the cafeteria, walking in the halls, waiting around in the parking lot for her ride home. Always at the center of a group of girls, the whole bunch of them chatting away nine to the dozen and giggling.

He disliked groups and he disliked girls who giggled too much. Even so, he thought, she seemed like one of the better ones. Never once poked fun at the way he spoke or dressed.

One day he caught her looking at him, so he asked one of her girlfriends about her. He learned that she volunteered at a shelter twice a week after school so he knew that she was kind. She had long dark hair and a pale complexion. He thought she was pretty. It was the cute ones that scared him the most.

He was neither nor cute nor kind, though he was gentle in manner and soft spoken. As a small boy, he liked to trap butterflies and pull the wings off them. His teachers would later describe him as gifted. The jerks called him a queer. In truth, none of them knew jack squat about him.

The two of them were what they were.

About three months ago, Debbie had started showing up again in his life. He saw her on the street. Serving up food at the place where he slept. Standing in a line at the bus station where he kept his things. Always at a distance. And when he tried to approach her, she'd be gone. Like a human mirage.

Now he found himself sitting across the desk from her in a dingy little office at the back of some fleabag all-night supermarket.

"Hi, I'm Debbie. Perhaps we could start with your name, Mr. . . ."

So she didn't recognize him! Or perhaps she did and she was pretending not to. Forgetting can be a boon sometimes. It was a skill he had spent most of his life trying to acquire. A remark, a sideways glance, a glimpse of untanned flesh, they were all right there for him front and center. Part of his process. Like a reverse case of Alzheimer's.

"Spivak. Michael Spivak. They call me Mike."

She looked him over.

"Right you are, Mike. Seems you have all the qualifications for this position."

It was said with a wry grin. He had seen an ad at the front of the store HELP NEEDED INQUIRE INSIDE and walked in, it was that type of job.

"It's a part-time appointment. Pays $9.75 an hour. You'll be stocking shelves, sweeping, that sort of thing. We'll need your services three times a week. Monday through Wednesday. You'll work the graveyard shift. I'm the manager here, I'll be your supervisor."

That day outside the Walgreens.

Hi, I'm Debbie. We're both in Ms. Fraser's class.

"No benefits, but the company does offer a supplemental health plan. It's optional. If you're interested, Linda in HR can fill you in on the details."

How she had styled her hair in pigtails. The blush in her cheeks. The curve of her breast. The curl of her mouth when she smiled at him and the way her front teeth stuck out a little, adding a sort of chipmunk like quality to her face. It was all there, locked away in some subterranean closet in his brain.

I know a place we could go, he told her.

I've got Twinkies in my bag, she replied.

"The lunchroom is out back. There are vending machines and a Keurig. You'll need to bring your own pods, of course."

How they had loved each other, that day in the woods. Stealing a few moments of joy among the briars and the ferns.

When it was done, they shared their plans. He was going to be an Electrical Engineer or a college professor.

I want to go to State. Study Biology, she said.

She was looking dreamy and picking daisies.

I wish we could stay this way forever, he said, stroking her face.

Then he lowered his hands to her throat and squeezed the life out of her.

"Did I mention the health plan?"

A taste in his mouth, an odor. The angle of the sunlight through the trees. The way her body jerked and twisted under him. Hands like hooks clawing at his eyes.

"As I said before, I'm the one that you will answer to."

He'd paid for what he had done. He'd paid plenty. What more did she want from him, after all these years? Didn't she know that there was nothing left alive inside him to give?

He wanted nothing better than to pick up and run out of there because at root, he was a coward. Didn't have the moxie to do even that, it seemed. And he knew, as she looked at him and smiled that toothy little smile, that he never would.

The things you did to people, big and small. They always came back to haunt you. And Debbie was one of the best.

"So, if there are no questions, Mr. Mike…"

She passed a set of papers across the desk and asked when he could start.

Monday, he said as he signed on the dotted line.

Double Take

James looked out of the window and shivered, and not just at the wintry London sky. After a month of preparation and planning, he had closed a major deal this afternoon. One that could impact his future with this firm, perhaps his entire career.

James glanced at the clock on his desk. Almost time for the call with his opposite number across the pond. He reached into his desk for a little something to steady his nerves. Her Royal Highness chose this moment to honor him with an appearance.

"The bad Penny! Been waiting all afternoon for one to turn up. *If* you catch my drift."

Penny was afraid that she did. She gave James a stony look. "I've just been on with Clare at A & T."

Penny was a Senior Assistant with the firm. Sharp and efficient, and serious to the point of scary. In all the time they had worked together, James could not recall the woman once smiling in his direction, though she seemed enough with the other women in the division— a circumstance from which James had not failed to draw a conclusion. In certain moments, James pictured Penny as a dominatrix named Helga. *Helga on with Clare* and *A & T...*

"They have to cancel their 5:00 pm. Some sort of medical situation involving Frank Greene."

"Medical situation, my aunt Fanny. Fellow probably decided he wanted the afternoon off to play golf. Or whatever it is they do to amuse themselves over there."

"She did sound quite upset."

James yawned and reached behind himself in an attempt to massage the tension from his back. He studied Penny across the desk. Decided that she looked like he felt.

"Oh well, I daresay we could both do with an early day."

James walked around the desk and made to place an arm around Penny's shoulders, a misery loves company sort of gesture. Penny shrugged the arm off like a petulant schoolgirl and headed for the door. "I'll be here until 5:30 if you need me."

***

Sleazy banter and touching again! Penny didn't linger there a second longer than necessary. It was so incredibly tiresome. Mother would no doubt have advised that she humor him.

Men are such silly creatures, dear…

Life is hard for a woman on her own. A girl needs to make the most of her natural advantages...

But Penny wasn't that type of girl and mother wasn't here anymore.

***

Penny had never known her father, who supposedly had abandoned her and her mother soon after she was born, but as a kid she had idolized her mother. Used to dream of following in her footsteps and becoming an actress. Something which, as the older woman never seemed to tire of pointing out—especially when things were less than harmonious between the two of them—she had been before fate had stepped in in the form of Penny's arrival in the world.

It seemed so romantic. Though she later discovered that the acting career had consisted of bit parts in a few TV commercials, Penny's child brain had conjured up pictures of a mansion in Hollywood, hordes of adoring fans, handsome princes in love with her, the works.

The fantasy worked well—up until the time Penny started to suspect what her mother really did for a living. *Suspected*, she was never quite sure. One thing Penny did know for sure, mummy had a lot of friends back then and they were all men. They would come to the house at night wearing dark suits and frozen smiles and always left before dawn. Like vampires.

Very nice to Penny, the men were. Provided she was a good little girl, minded her p's and q's, and stayed out of the way. Then, one night when her mother had popped out of the house to pick up "something she needed" *Talk to Uncle Joe luv, while I'm gone. Show him the picture you pained at school today* one of them had...

Penny didn't feel much like a movie star these days. She had fallen into a pit long ago and there were no handsome princes, only snakes. The councilor said it would take time, that she needed to learn to trust. Penny heard the clock ticking as she lay awake at night and felt the pulse throbbing in her throat and thought she didn't have that much—time or trust.

A few weeks ago, she had met someone. A recent addition to her weekly therapy group. An awkward, sad-eyed man, looked to be around her age, perhaps a few years older. Social anxiety, she heard, possible Asperger's. Whatever, this man had stirred something new and strange in Penny. Penny was unsure quite what to do with this. As a human being, you were supposed to be able to feel, or what was the point of it all. And yet...

Would he be there again tonight, this man? What would they find to say to each other, anyway? She was hardly the assertive type and he had not shown any particular interest in her.

***

James Flynn had been with the firm of *Foster-Sloan* almost five years. His rise through the ranks had been nothing short of meteoric, all things considered. Nonetheless, he hadn't made a major killing in almost a year, and the word was that his career had stalled. If he were to achieve the goal he had set himself of making Partner by the age of forty, he would need to pull off something big, and soon. This Abernathy deal might just be the one.

Not if it blew up in his face! You could get a pass on just about anything in this game, it seemed. Cronyism, double dealing, creative billing, embezzlement even, provided you did it in style and you had the right friends. The one thing they never forgave—BAD JUDGEMENT. The pokey outside offices and the cubicles were rank with the stink of dead ambition. Burned out husks in the twilight of their careers begging scraps from the tables of the...

What had he done?

James' mind began to wander as it was wont to do lately, back to his student days. Why was he drawn to that time of all times at times like this? There was something in there that seemed important somehow, but for the life of him he could never figure out *what,* or why.

Was it because he was happy then? It seemed unlikely. Broke, strung out, living on the edge, cheap booze and cheap women and whatever else the hell he could lay his hands on, just to make it through from one day to the next. And all the darned studying! Keynes and Marx—a bunch of medieval junk that no one in the business world even cared about these days—just to keep one step ahead of the curve.

Funny to think how once he had been on the point of throwing it all in the crapper and taking up, of all things—bartending! James shuddered at the thought.

***

The wind was picking up and it was starting to snow. Sam had polished off the last of his thermos of coffee a half-hour ago and it felt like his lips were starting to freeze.

Sam peered through the newly cleaned window, admiring his handiwork. There was a man inside looking at his computer. Sam noted with some amusement that the bloke actually looked a lot like him! Or he would do minus the Van Dyke, the fancy suit and about twenty pounds around the midriff.

The man turned his head in the direction of the window and Sam looked away. They weren't supposed to look in the windows and he needed this job.

Up here, Sam had plenty of time to think. Days like this he mainly thought that he should have stayed in school. He was a student at the famous *London School of Economics*. He could have become something, somebody. The professors all told him he had the smarts. The world at his fingertips, the future his. *Grab it*, they said.

How could he grab the future when he couldn't even make sense of his past? One morning, he dozed off on the bus after spending the whole night in the school library. Found his sorry self in South Kensington without a penny to get home and decided then and there that he might like pulling pints more than he liked pulling all-nighters. Twenty years on and here he was.

Sam looked at the man again. Remarkable, really, the resemblance! Downright freaky, in fact. Right down to the mole on the right side of his (their) face!

Sam stared through the window, open mouthed and no longer amused.

***

It was hot in the office and James' sinuses were starting to act up. As he turned his head to grab for a box of tissues, something at the edge of his vision caught his attention. He looked up at the window.

There was a window cleaner on a scaffold out there. The man was looking at him. Not looking— staring! The man looked away the instant they made eye contact. The prospect of corporate espionage reared its ugly head. Perhaps the fellow had one of those tiny high-resolution cameras? James adjusted the position of his computer screen so that it faced away from the window.

The Abernathy figures stared at him, taunting him. Sucker, they seemed to say, we got *your* number this time!

Right now, James would gladly have traded places with the window cleaner. No more market analyses, actuarial tables, stock projections, senior partners...

In spite of what he had said to Penny about leaving early, James knew that he wouldn't get out of here for at least another two hours. There was a report to work up on this Abernathy affair, due on old man Foster's desk by start of business tomorrow. After that he was home free. Free to return home to his Mayfair flat and stare at the four walls and think about the pair of concrete boots he had fashioned for himself this day.

Spies posing as window cleaners and concrete boots. James wondered what that high-priced shrink of his would make of it. He was so tired. Tired from a grand total of ten hours of sleep in the past three days. Tired of this firm. Most of all, tired of himself.

James laid his head on the desk and thought about Penny. Thought that she was hot. Or she would be if she weren't so freaking cold. No problem, he would thaw her out. Melt her heart and make her his forever. S J. Flynn, Esq., knight in shining armor. He could do anything, right?

In your dreams, hotshot, he thought as he drifted off. *In another universe...*

***

Sam shrugged and glanced at his watch. Time to pack it in for the day. Just as well, not only was he freezing his tail off up here, he was seeing doubles! He would hit the pub on the way home for a pint and a spot of supper. Then go home and crash in front of the TV. Business as usual.

Well, not quite. With a little jolt of anticipation, Sam remembered that today was Thursday. Tonight was the weekly meeting of the support group he had recently started attending. There was a woman in the group that he was attracted to, though she was no doubt way out of his league. They'd only spoken a few times. She told him that her name was Penny and that she lived alone since her mother died and worked as a secretary for an investment company in the city. And that she hated vampires.

Sam looked at the man again. He had his head down on the desk now. Some sweet gig, paid through the nose to sleep half the day in his plush warm office. Sam didn't envy the man, though. Fact was, he liked this job well enough, sub-arctic conditions and all. Up here in the sky he felt free. No boss to push him around, no snotty customers to deal with, no smart-mouthed coworkers making his life miserable. Just Samuel James Flynn, perched above the world like an eagle.

Sam's thoughts returned to Penny. It had been so long since he had been with a woman. By all indications, she was unattached. He had been trying to work up the courage to ask her out. He'd do it tonight if the opportunity presented itself. Definitely tonight, he hoped.

Twins

In the summer of 1989, Emily Simone gave birth to identical twins. Roger was in law school at the time. The joyous couple figured that since they had two exactly the same, and in the interest of both economy and public spiritedness, they might as well give one up. So they flipped a coin to decide which it would be.

Bonnie Crandall recently graduated from Purdue and is about to embark on a career as a high school Chemistry teacher. Tails Simone experienced some emotional problems, bouncing from counselor to counselor, job to job, eventually settling on a career in adult entertainment.

One day the two will almost meet, on a two-way escalator in a shopping mall in downtown Chicago, Bonnie going up and Tails going down. And stare disbelieving at each other for an instant, before parting ways again forever.

Fruit

"The pear-shaped doorman murmured a squishy good morning. Big purple face like a giant pomegranate. The man reminded Frank of Buster Higgs. Buster and his mob of...

Frank nodded curtly at the doorman, entered the marbled lobby and rode the elevator up to the tenth floor.

The drive to work had brought on another blinding headache. Frank walked over to the window and closed the shades, then fumbled in his desk for a bottle of aspirin.

Around 10:30, there came a knock on the door and Clare walked in. Clare was an Executive Assistant with the firm of *Ashe & Turner*. A pleasant young woman, smart and professional. At least, she had always *used* to be that way. Fact was, recently Clare had been messing up on the job. Mislaying documents. Playing silly pranks. Canceling meetings without his say so. Changing things up in his office when he was gone and pretending no knowledge of it.

"I scheduled Foster for noon in 8.21."

Her behavior of late had become so bizarre, so darned inappropriate at times, that Frank was almost inclined to believe that Clare was getting *fresh* with him. He a married man and this girl young enough to be his...

Well not quite, but almost.

"Can't this wait until tomorrow? A little tied up with this other nonsense right now. On second thoughts, have them make an appointment like everyone else. We're not Burger King."

Clare shot Frank one of her looks. "They already did. You approved it last week."

Frank was having a little trouble keeping track of things lately, but of this he was sure, he had approved no such thing.

"They only need twenty minutes."

Clare took note of Frank's complexion and hesitated a beat before going on.

"Do you want me to—

Somehow he didn't see her come around the desk but suddenly she was all over him, yelling in his ear.

— for you?"

"What the… WHAT IN GOD'S NAME ARE YOU DOING, WOMAN?"

"It looked like you needed some… something. "

Needed some something!

"That's what you thought, is it?"

The poor girl looked frightened. Had be overreacted?

"Didn't mean to snap, sweetie, but… *really*!"

Frank stood up and offered a smile and a reassuring arm. Clare flinched at the touch and skipped over to the other side of the desk. Stood there gawking at him.

Frank had recently started to see people as produce. The sweet looking boy in the mailroom was a peach. His housekeeper Mrs. Womack had become a Granny Smith. The weird new Assistant in Accounting who always looked so sour was a gooseberry, and now Clare stood before him as a Golden Delicious.

Clare handed over a thin sheath of papers. "The agenda for the Board meeting and your schedule of afternoon appointments. I'm out of here. Buzz me if you need anything."

Bite me, is what Frank heard.

***

Clare didn't linger there a second longer than necessary. She didn't know what the heck was going on with Frank, but he was freaking the living daylights out of her. One minute he's carrying on a normal conversation—or what passed for normal in the Frank universe these days—and the next gone AWOL. Just as she's on the point of calling in the medics, he's back on planet earth and yelling at her and the next instant all smiles and good cheer.

She had nearly jumped out of her skin when he touched her. You'd think she'd be getting used to it by now, this was the third such episode in as many weeks. Mood swings, lapses of memory, temper tantrums. Her mom had acted a bit like this when she went through the 'pause, but such female angst hardly jived with the testosterone-soaked world of corporate finance.

A mid-life crisis? After five years in this place, Clare thought she knew all about that too and again it didn't seem to fit. She wondered if Frank was undergoing a mental breakdown.

***

The air in the office was thick as molasses and Frank's body felt slow and heavy. It had been a while since he had taken the aspirin and the headache was making a comeback. Everything around him seemed stretched and sort of wobbly, as though he were observing the world from underwater. And he was finding it increasingly hard to get his thoughts going in the right direction. The crap that was set to come down on his head this afternoon. Clare and her antics. That boy downstairs making doe eyes at him again. The way young people carried on these days! Last night Rosie had left him. Taken his little cherry and his strawberry with her. Something to do with the way *he* was acting, for God's sake! And not even the decency to tell him where she was going!

Frank screwed up his eyes against the sheer unfairness of it all. Pictured a Roman orgy, silver platters stacked with human entrails.

First come, first served…

Solid predictable Frank smiled slyly to himself. He was becoming creative in his old age! *Perhaps they'll sign me on as writer for of those late-night movies.*

Right now, there was something more pressing to worry about. The boys from downtown would be descending on his doorstep not two hours from now.

Nothing to be alarmed about, sport. Just need to have a little chat about these reports we've been receiving.

Sport!? There were files to be retrieved before then. Memos to be tracked down. Items that would establish beyond a shadow of a doubt that he had indeed submitted those... It was all so exhausting.

He wished his dad were here.

Strange, he hadn't thought about the man in so long. It's just that these days he felt so lame. Unmanly, almost…

"FRUITY FR— "

This infernal headache! On and off now for three straight days. If he could only lose it, then perhaps he could start to pull it all back together. He figured they had to be at her mother's. He would drive across town the minute he got through here and reclaim them. The way he felt right now, he doubted he would make it across the room. And the goons from Head Office were on the way. A grapefruit and a prickly pear. *Nothing to be alarmed about, sport.*

Frank looked at the schedule of afternoon appointments that Clare had left. The call with London at noon. At 3:00, his weekly report to the Bowl of Prunes. It needed more work. He was going to have to rewrite that whole section on…

Frank realized with a gasp of horror that he had no idea what the report was about! *Was he losing his mind?* He'd been working on the damn thing for two days!

Frank rifled through his notes looking for a clue. None of it made sense.

***

It felt as though Frank's head was about to explode. He must have fallen asleep. The clock on his desk had advanced by leaps and bounds and his laptop was lying face down on the floor.

There was something he needed to do. What, he had no idea, except that it was unpleasant and apparently involved something green and prickly and a round sour thing.

There was a ringing sound in his ears and a nasty smell in the air, like a mixture of burning rubber and manure. And it was so hot in here, you could have fried an egg on his forehead.

It occurred to Frank that perhaps there was a fire in the building. Scenes from the movie *Towering Inferno* came spilling into his head. His father had taken to see it when he was a kid. He remembered the occasion like it was yesterday. He remembered being happy that day. It was a Sunday, the day before his dad had left him and his mom. His dad had played football in high school, had wanted Frank to play. If he hadn't been such a little wimp then perhaps...

There's no smoke without fire and smoke is what Frank smelled now. He could hear shouting in the distance, faint now but becoming louder by the second...

Chaos and mayhem were erupting everywhere on the upper floors of the building. People acting like animals, yelling and shoving, trampling each other in a vain effort to get to safety. Rotten bananas, the whole damn bunch of them.

Close by, an elevator (perhaps the very same one Frank had ridden up in that morning) packed full with screaming people crashed to the ground. There was a warning sign to USE STAIRS IN THE EVENT OF FIRE, but the stairwell was blocked and in any case it seemed people rarely paid attention to warning signs these days. Especially the people in *this* elevator who, as it now turned out, were all either anonymous or despicable. One jerk had actually pulled a woman out of the cab just before the doors closed and jammed himself in there in her place! This jerk also had the face of Buster Higgs.

Well, he got his! Frank thought gleefully.

Frank was fourteen years old and sitting in the Warner Cineplex, staring transfixed at the flickering screen and munching on popcorn. Buster and his gang of dorks called him FRUITY FRANCIS. There had been a thing with a boy in the tenth grade, but they wouldn't dare call him that now. Not if they could see him with Rose and Mark and Anne. His position with the firm. The way that Clare… Anyway, how could he be a fruit when he was sitting here watching a real scary grown-up movie and he was not feeling the least bit scared.

Best of all, his dad was being unusually nice to him today. He took him to see this movie and bought him popcorn *and* a hot dog! It was going to be alright, after all!

Frank took a first bite of the hot dog. It was delicious, hot and juicy, oozing with mustard and ketchup. Frank sighed contentedly. He was safe here. Home at last after a long strange journey, or just a bad dream?

Only, this was all wrong. They closed the Warner down years ago and converted it into an apartment building. *Rose… Mark… Anne… Clare?* Who were these people? And what was "the firm?" Somewhere off in the distance a bell was ringing and his head hurt.

Suddenly, the pain in Frank's head escalated to the level of scalding agony and his vision exploded. He wanted to scream and couldn't. His eyes rolled back in his head as blackness washed over him and he was—

***

Clare glanced at the clock on her computer. 11:59 and Frank had still not emerged from his office. He was going to be late for his call on the eighth floor.

Clare knocked sharply on the door and entered anyway when there was no response.

The poor man must have been exhausted, he was sound asleep in his chair. He looked so helpless sitting there, just like a little boy, with his head thrown back and his mouth wide open. She hated to wake him but he was late for his call.

Troll Bot[1]

[1] *Troll Bot*: a device that monitors Internet traffic, searching for suspicious activity.

The latest item had come in while Ray was out of the office. TB17 West Coast. Ray looked at it and swore under his breath. He hadn't signed on for this crap, at least it wasn't what he thought he was signing on for. Looked like he was in for the duration now. No official rule against resigning of course, yet you heard things...

Ray shuddered, he had a couple of kids. He forced his attention back to the printout.

Awaiting Cat:
8/15/2015 9:35 am PST
tombo3574/gmail.com

OUR STREET

ON OUR STREET every chylde has one momm and one ddad
ON OUR STREET everybody is wyte
Everybody is strate
Everybody sez their prerz
Dogz live forever
Catz don't exist
Everybody bavz twice a day
ON OUR STREET everybody is **DEDD**

What the frack, a *poem*? Following this "work of art," the usual synopsis. Ray felt a little sick as he read it over.

Tamas (Tommy) Oleinic
Age: 15
Caucasian male
Father: Krystof
Mother: Yelena
Parents divorced, no sibs
Address: 355 Post Street, Portland OR 83510 (Mother's res.)
St Johns High School, Oak Hill District, Portland OR

Introvert/extrovert Spectrum: L2. (No friends or close acquaintances identified.)
Grades: B/C (underachiever)
Sexual orientation: unknown
Affiliations: Robotics Club
Crim: n/a
Psy: n/a

Chad looked over from the other desk, seemingly bored in spite of himself. "Whatcha got there, Buster?"

Ray looked back stonily. At forty-five years of age, he must be ten years older than this schmuck, though the other man had seniority. He was welcome to it.

Ray handed it over. "Came in ten minutes ago."

"Hmm… The names all sound Eastern European. Most likely why it got picked up… after Boston."

"Kid sounds like a goddam halfwit, if you ask me."

Chad shook his head and favored Ray with his *expert* smile.

"*Nerd,* garden variety. Loner. Disaffected, with poetic inclinations. Type they stick KICK ME signs on the back of. Type that feels he needs to make a STATEMENT."

Ray sighed. "Want me to send it on?"

"Fits the profile."

"Pretty darned weak, I'd say. See the Crim/Psy? C-4 at the most."

"We're sending C-4 now. You did get the memo, I suppose?"

"*High school kids,* for Christ's sake?"

Ray was thinking about Anne, who was majoring in Psychology at Penn State. About Mark, who would be applying to colleges this year. About the neighbor's kid who had gone missing just last week.

Chad thought about that little crackpot who had strangled his girlfriend over in Senna Woods and dumped her body in the lake. Quite a legend in these parts, he was. They still spoke about it fifteen years later.

"Hey, shit happens. Kid walks into a mall. *Say hello to my little friend.* Next thing you know we're on *Fox News Sunday.*"

"We are? I'll need to get a haircut."

"The department, wiseass. Wind up looking kind of bad. And when *that* happens..."

"Heads will roll."

"Always do when the S hits the F."

"Whereas a whack-job chemist in Atlanta turns up in a dumpster…"

"That's what you do with garbage, right?"

"A truck driver in Maine."

"Fell asleep at the wheel of his cab, if memory serves. Happens all the time."

"A nutty professor in South Carolina."

Chad gave a slow whistle and assumed his quiet voice.

"That was something, that was. All those poor people at that school. What you gonna do, slap the bastard on the wrist? Ship him off to some white-collar piss palace in Pleasantville? Touch football in the yard and conjugal visits every other weeken—"

"A witless little punk in Oregon?"

"Don't sweat it. Probably won't ever happen."

"If it does, we won't see it on Fox."

"Brief mention on *News at Ten,* perhaps. On a slow night."

"We all get a gold star."

"Hell, it's nice to be appreciated."

"Perhaps a bonus."

"Baby needs a new set of boots."

"You know what? I've just about had it with this shit."

"Hey you got a problem Joe Friday, take it upstairs. I'm just doing my job."

"Your job."

"Keeping the public safe."

Kill My Darling

Her story is called *Bones*. Published in *WOMBAT*, a literary rag based in Boston that also covers news and politics. I read it online, a classy looking outfit. *Must be*, I think with irony, given how they treated *Spring Fever*. Probably the best piece of flash I ever wrote.

I think about this, how you bleed yourself onto the page and they wipe you away. Took a whopping six weeks and not so much as a by-your-leave. I light up another smoke and pretend for a moment that I give a rat's ass about any of this crap anymore.

I bring up the two pieces and set them on the screen side by side. Weigh the one against the other. A tale about a kid and her dog, and my madness. We are defined by these themes, she and I, two sides of the same coin, the good versus the bad and the ugly.

Her latest offering, up there in a million pixels.

Read it, a voice that is not mine growls.

I already did.

You have to chew down on this one, the voice says. It's a little weird but then I haven't slept in three days.

Read it.

I have but little choice. I screw up my eyes against the glare of her words. Think I'll need to dash out the store and pick up a blindfold or else put out my eyes, it might be easier. I want to screw her words. They jump off the page and tear at my heart.

In front of me is her headshot, together with the usual 50-word bio and a link to her Facebook page. A cute young thing, looks like butter wouldn't melt. Huge fan of the beat poets and the films of David Lynch and the music of The Clash. Has an aunt who is also a writer, and works part time as a waitress at a Chili's downtown.

None of it is news to me. You see, I know her too well, this woman. I was her in a previous life. I see her at the Y with her three-year old, watch them playing together in the pool. Listen to the shrieks and the squeals. I think about the way my own child died. Maybe I'll visit her one night.

Placebo

My doctor prescribes a drug for my heart condition. She tells me it is a placebo and should start working in two to three months.

Early Closing

Days like this, when time seemed to stand still. When you learned to turn your mind off and drift away. Think about Big Macs. Chimpanzees. Sundials. Anything but Brian. The way he smiled. The way he looked when they found him...

Parker's convenience store stands at the edge of Granet, Texas along a dusty stretch of State Road 380. The name of the town is pronounced "granite." It was founded by a French Huguenot in the early 1700s, who fled his native land to escape religious persecution.

Albie took stock of the day. It had been alright, he supposed. Hot as hell, but better than most. Albie works at the store three hours after school on weekdays and all-day Saturdays. He is a gentle boy, seventeen years of age. He lives with his widowed mother in a dilapidated farmhouse some three miles from the store.

None of the jerks had messed with him, at least.

The store is managed by a rotund bespectacled gentleman in his mid-forties. A jolly sort. Toastmaster, scout leader, lay preacher at First Baptist in town when opportunity presents. The manager has been married twenty years and is bored with his wife and with life in general.

Only, something felt wrong.

The manager had put the CLOSED sign on the front door a little earlier than usual and locked it, and was standing at the cash register counting bills. The other two sales staff had left for the day. Albie was stocking shelves.

Looking behind him, he quickly figured out what it was. *Just the two of them here.* He shot a glance at the clock on the wall. Twenty more minutes until he could leave.

The manager left his place behind the counter. He was coming over here. Standing directly behind him.

As a kid the manager used to dream of being a war hero, but he was too young for Nam. By the time the Gulf War rolled around he was disqualified for health reasons—type 2 diabetes and high blood pressure. Had entertained plans by the bushel—pilot, cattle rancher, stunt man, Billy Graham and Dirty Harry all rolled into one, but the wrong crowd and a little foolishness in his younger days had landed him a spell as a guest of the state, and you learned a thing or two in a place like that. And this boy and his reputation stirred the wicked in him and he was the kind of man who liked to express his feelings.

Albie expected some instruction—more beans on the second shelf, or refill the Twizzlers. But none came. Instead, the manager smacked the flat of his hand against Albie's right buttock. Wrapped thick arms around his waist and grabbed at his belt buckle.

"GOTCHA, sweet stuff!"

The insult to his rear. The hands on his body. The stink of stale sweat and rancid cigar breath. The manager had made a few strange remarks to him in the past week, given him funny looks, even tried to touch him once, but this was too much. He wrenched free of the man's grip and spun around.

Face to face in the empty store, they might have been the last two creatures left on earth. Albie shrank back against the shelves. Felt his throat constrict, the flesh on his back tighten, as though his body was trying to shrink inside itself.

"*Don't.*"

The manager moved a step closer. Albie pushed him away. The manager was unoffended, he liked a little spunk.

"We can do this the easy way or the hard way, boy. I know which one I prefer."

Albie was fourteen when his father passed away from prostate cancer. He thought the way his father died, the yellow smell of the sick room. Thought about his classmates. About what happened last month. The teachers and the guidance counselor. The strange way they all looked at him now. *STUPID STUPID STUPID* screamed the voice inside his head for letting himself get suckered into this...

Meanwhile, the manager was in the mood to party. Pawing. Slapping. Dancing him up and down the aisle. Puckering up his lips and making clucking sounds in his ear as though the two of them were a pair of chickens.

Albie was a slightly built boy born under the sign of Pisces, yet lately a power raged inside him that was terrible and ugly. He would burn this creep alive. Beat him with whips and chains. Give him stage four and listen to him as he shouted night after night in his bed and pissed himself. Take him out to an abandoned warehouse and string him up from the rafters, and hoot and holler alongside a gang of hoodlums as he thrashed his guts out. Do it all tonight as he sat in his room at home with his comic books and his Nintendo and the heat inside him and the voices screaming and tell himself that it wasn't himself that he really hated.

A week or a month down the road, a different voice would tell him that it didn't much matter, that thing in the store. Just another sweaty old day in Granet, Texas, the voice would say.

A day in the life of a…

Albie thought about his friend. The way he smiled.

The way he looked when they found him…

There must have been a blow, though Albie was hardly aware of having struck one. His right fist had turned a livid shade of red and the joints were starting to blacken and swell. The manager was on the floor.

Albie stepped into the office and picked up his jacket. As he was about to leave the store he paused to cast a final glance back at the manager. The man had risen to his knees and was staring up at him with an air of befuddled disbelief. His jaw looked all wrong, and he was holding out a hand as though in a gesture of supplication.

Outside, the air was filled with the sound of chirping crickets. The sunset had painted the sky in swirling spirals of purple and gold. A cool breeze blowing in from the North brought the scent of lotus blossom.

Portrait of a Genius

The old man sits stiffly in the ornately carved chair, lush satin robes flowing off straight broad shoulders. The position of the head and the set of the jaw truculent, determined, rigid to the core. The set of the double chin arrogant. The cast of the watery blue eyes under white unkempt brows kindly and soft. But this is illusory, for there is nothing of either quality about this man. On closer inspection, a tangled web of emotions can be read in the eyes: frustration, pride, contempt, satisfaction, resignation, triumph, despair…

A childless man with ten thousand heirs. His life stretches behind him like a beam of light focused through a lens, the focal point the instant he determined he was different to the mortals among whom he was cast; immune to their weaknesses, vices, vicissitudes, hopes, joys… *The instant of his birth.*

He reflects on the days when he was a king, a usurper, a maker and a destroyer of worlds. The outpouring of pure creative power, a raw naked fury. Had he been born in another place or time he might have become a great general or an ingenious multiple killer.

The enemies are all gone now. The hunchback and the cripple and the clown. The petty detractors and the spoilers. The falsifiers and the pretenders. The dabblers in low magic. One by one, turned to dust.

The days of glory are gone, too. The academies love him but commoners don't show him the respect he deserves. Street urchins dog his steps and pull ugly faces, then flee in mock terror when he turns around to confront them. Tradesmen mistake him for a servant. The waiter at the club where he dines shows him to the table by the kitchens, out of the sight of "gentlemen."

What does he care? His place is at the head of kings.

The beam is fading fast now as the pain in his chest builds to a fine crescendo. Finally, an adversary worthy of respect, a friend even.

Still time to set down a few final thoughts, something for the mindless hordes to pore over later. Scrutinize. *Analyze,* in the nonsensical prattle of the day. No doubt they'll conclude that he hated his father and had designs on his mother. He reflects that they may be on to something with the first part of that. As for the second… he giggles like a small child. Perhaps he'll write something along those lines, a last act of comic defiance from a man they say is humorless. Then again, perhaps he won't.

The old man dips quill in ink one last time and sits back in the chair, unbowed and imperious even now. A creator and a destroyer, a bringer of light to the world. *Diva* and *Shiva* and *Ra.* A genius or a god or a lunatic.

Just the Two of Us

Yes, there are two of us. *Julie and Sarah.* We look alike on the outside, but *inside...*

Sarah is like cotton candy—after you've stuffed yourself with it at the fair. Laughs a lot at pictures of cats and babies that she sees online, even has her own Facebook page. Julie doesn't do any of that crap.

Julie is the cleverer of the two. Julie knows everything that Sarah knows and a whole lot more besides. Enough to know that Sarah is wacko! A real nut job. Brushes her teeth and washes her hands about a hundred times a day. Wipes the posts in the schoolyard. *Weak.* Lets the brats poke fun. Worries herself silly about stupid things like the world oil situation and the fate of the panda population and people she knows dying.

Julie never worries about anything, and she's not big on furry things and she spits on clean. But then again, she's not the one who is crazy. So she just watches it all from afar and she bides her time. And every day she grows a little stronger.

***

Sarah is very quiet now and she spends a lot of time crying in her room. Julie is a holy terror. Their poor put upon mother and their teachers don't get it. Nobody does.

Sarah. Sarah. Sarah. Sarah. Always Sarah.

She used to be so sweet, they say.

***

So here she is in the background for yet another "consultation." *Julie.* Perched on a wooden stool in a corner of the room like the place they put her after she beat up that kid. Sarah is back home locked in the cupboard underneath the sink where Julie left her after she tied her up and gagged her.

There is nothing better to do in this place so Julie runs her fingernails up and down her arms as she rocks back and forth on the stool. Bloodies them a little because she hasn't cut her nails in a while. Twists her face into a pretzel. Thinks about dirtying herself because she wants to give them shit. Except it doesn't feel like that's on the cards right now so she just sits there rocking. Back and forth, back and forth, she goes, back and forth, in tidy groups of threes, raking her arms with her nails once in between each round because parity is all and nothing works for her like odd.

After a while she grows bored with this game, so she gets up and she wanders into their circle. She is invisible to them so she can go just anywhere she wants. And catch some of the whispered conversation, because when you're invisible you're deaf too.

As they're about to get into the car the yelling and the twenty questions start up.

WHAT DID YOU DO NOW?

If you carry on like this they are going to lock you away. Is that what you want?

A single parent nightmare. Every day a struggle!

Why do you do this to me?

But on the way home they stop by Dairy Queen and her mother buys her chicken nuggets and a shake, and the two of them share it. And for a short time there is only mom and Sarah.

Fragments

Jerry watched her as she slept. Eyes like almonds, pale skin, long black hair splayed against the white pillow. Jerry was a connoisseur of art. He loved to watch her like this. Luanne muttered something unintelligible and turned over. What was she dreaming about?

***

"I wanted you so bad."

"When?"

"That night after the movie."

"You seemed so distant. Closed up. It would have felt like intruding."

"Am I so hard to read?"

"These days my near vision isn't too good."

***

Jerry looked at the clock on the bedside table for the umpteenth time. 4:35 a.m. He climbed out of bed and walked over to the bookshelf. Picked out a book and opened it to the photograph of his favorite work of sculpture. He had seen the real thing once. As a young man, on a trip to Paris with his mother. The sculpture had embarrassed him then. Supposedly it depicted a scene from Dante's Inferno. Two lovers locked in an embrace at the gates of hell.

***

They were leaving a movie theater after watching the first hour of a Hungarian film. There was a scene in the film where a man was visiting his wife in the hospital. The wife had attempted suicide after being forced by the husband into getting an abortion when she became pregnant with a third child that the couple could not afford. Luanne had become agitated and insisted that they leave.

"Why did you take me to see that piece of shit?" she demanded as they were getting into his car.

"I'm so sorry," Jerry mumbled. "I didn't think…
It won an award at Cannes."

They didn't speak again the rest of the evening.

Later that night, she came to his bed. She didn't seem to want anything, just to feel the warmth of another human body.

***

Jerry suddenly felt very tired. He replaced the book on the shelf and turned around, ready to get back into bed.

Luanne was standing there. She had tears in her eyes and she looked much older, around the age that Jerry's mother had been when she died. It didn't occur to Jerry to ask why she was crying.

What he did say was, "You are so beautiful, Rodin would have wanted you as a model."

Luanne turned her face away and replied in his mother's voice, *What did you take from me?*

Family Relations

I'm almost out, I said, *may I borrow your adapter again?*

I was talking about my laptop. My power brick had fried itself a couple of days ago and I had been making use of hers since she has the same type. *She* is my sister-in-law, my wife's sister. We were all staying with my in-laws for a while, at their place in the Texas hill country. Three of us, wife, sister-in-law, yours truly, were seated around a table in a trailer attached to the property.

Last night, it got hot in here.

Uncomfortably so, I said.

She disconnected her power source from the wall and slid it across the table.

I've ordered him another one, it should arrive on Friday. Wife.

So he's like twelve years old, he can't order his own stuff? I always do mine.

Yes, but then you have more time on your hands. Wife again. She gave her sister a puzzled look. *And you don't have a honey to do it for you.*

When you're done with it, you can slide it back over. Don't come over here.

I shoved the thing straight back at her.

On second thoughts, I said, *I think I'll wait till Friday.*

The evening before. I came into the trailer to fetch a bottle of wine from the refrigerator. Sister-in-law was sitting at the table poring over some plans she was drawing up for a house she was thinking of building on the land here, where she intended to retire eventually.

This is how it played out.

Hey, take a look at the hallway. I'm thinking of putting in a spiral staircase.

I walked over to the table to look at the plans.

That could work. More space efficient.

I studied the overall layout and decided that I liked the economy of the design. I'm a builder by trade so I know a little something about this type of thing.

Ever consider a second career as an architect?

She scowled at this, as though I was poking fun. She used to be a dancer with an avant-garde theater troupe.

This would be the place to seat it, I reckon.

I picked up a pencil and made a mark on the paper to indicate the section of the hall where I thought the staircase should go.

Whoa, buddy, not so free with my things. And while we're on the subject, BACK OFF SOME, will you?

I took a couple of steps back, confused and a little wounded. Then I cottoned to the problem, or so I thought. We had agreed when we arrived here that we would social distance, as much as is possible with a handful of people hanging out together for a month in one place.

Oh, you mean the virus thing.

It's not that. I feel threatened.

By me?

Well, yeah.

Threatened how, exactly?

Come on man, don't do that. I know you two have been having... marital issues lately and don't think I don't see the way you've been eyeing me up.

Marital issues. I wondered what the heck the two of them had been discussing in their late-night confabulations out here.

And eyeing her up? I stared dumbly at her.

Now you barge in on me when I'm in here alone, with your smarmy wisecracks and a look in your eyes like you haven't had it in...

Then, suddenly, lord help us, her hand was on my crotch.

My sister-in-law and I had known each other most of our adult lives. My wife and I drove a thousand miles across country for her wedding and she served as matron of honor at ours. She was there for us when my wife miscarried, and there to share in our joy when our son was born. And we would all spend as much time as possible with each other at the yearly family reunions and other occasions. Through good and bad, dealings between the two of us had never been other than righteous. I should have got out of there fast, only I didn't.

A short while later, my sister-in-law was diagnosed with something inoperable. Dizziness and fainting spells. At first, she worried that she was pregnant. My wife cried solidly for a day and a half when she learned the prognosis: lapses of memory, loss of coordination and bladder control, impaired judgment. Alteration in personality typified by episodes of passive/aggressive and in some cases, violent or promiscuous behavior. The little family gathering in Texas would be the last.

Then my wife left me. We never once spoke about the incident and it's unclear quite when and how she learned about it. Yet there was no doubt that she knew. It was there in her eyes, her voice.

Now I live alone and I revisit my marriage again and again. The time when we were happy and then the time when we weren't. There were problems before and there were problems after, but it always seems that the dividing point between the two was that night in the trailer. Naturally, I think about this too, her sickness and my weakness. Our combined madness. I don't think I'll ever be able to forgive myself for that. What I think about most though is not the night, but the next day. The way we were with each other as we sat at that table, one at each end with my poor wife in the middle.

The believers will tell you that someday the three of us will sit together at a different table and on that day we will figure out a way to make peace with ourselves and each other.

Somehow, I doubt it.

Mulgravia

General

The principality of *Mulgravia* is located in the foothills of the Ural Mountains and occupies approximately 8.5 square miles of land. The official population is 9,357 according to the latest census conducted in 2005, but the figure could be misleading as it is thought that up to 15% of households may not have returned the form. [1]

Mulgravia possesses a remarkable physical characteristic. It is situated between landforms in such a way as to be virtually invisible from outside. Perhaps for this reason the country is cloaked in a shroud of anonymity. The principality appears on no world maps, is never featured in foreign travelogues, nor is the subject of questions on trivia shows in foreign lands.

Indeed, a strange psychological mechanism appears to hold sway. People the world over seem unaware of Mulgravia's existence until some unusual circumstance brings it to the fore, then tend to forget about it as soon as said circumstance is passed. Some even maintain that the country is a myth, like the lost city of Atlantis. Perhaps for this reason, Mulgravia has been largely ignored by the rest of the world throughout much of its history. [2] This has proven advantageous at times. The country remained untouched by the many wars that swept through Europe and served as a refuge [3] during WWII for Jews and other targets of Nazi persecution.

Religion

Mulgravia has likewise avoided incursions from religious groups. Crusaders, Jihadists and missionaries never came to the land. As a result, mainstream religion never took root there. Instead, many of the people follow an ancient homegrown system of beliefs known as *Luvetsk* (a term that loosely translates to "life essence"). The doctrine is nature-based, reminiscent of some Native American tribes combined with Druidic elements.

Military

The Mulgravian military has two branches, Army and Air Force (since the country is landlocked there is no Navy). The Army, consisting mostly of volunteer reservists, conducts training exercises every other weekend. The chief drawing card is the uniforms, which are said to be the most ornate in the whole of Europe. The Air Force operates on a similar basis. It has recently acquired a fleet of helicopters and is training a squad of pilots to fly them.

An intense rivalry exists between Army and Air Force focused largely on the uniforms. This situation resulted in a duel with pistols in 1903 between the heads of the two branches, Marshal Gunnar Koch and Wing Admiral Viktor Tietze, in which the Marshal was fatally wounded and the Wing Admiral killed outright. To diffuse tensions, the heads of the two branches are now required to dine together twice a year in civilian dress and with no side arms.

The Mulgravia Color Guard, founded in 1293 as bodyguard to the Royal Family is still in existence today although its function nowadays is purely ceremonial. The eight standing members of the Guard parade outside the Royal Palace and hire themselves out at pageants and other festivals, where they provide demonstrations of crossbow shooting.

Economy

A major source of revenue is Pyrite, a rich vein of which was discovered in the north of the country in the early 1900s.

Mulgravia has been involved in several commercial operations including whaling and overseas banking.

For a time, Mulgravian camouflage passports were manufactured by a group based in Chechnya. The operation was shut down after protests by the Mulgravian ruling family and after the passports were discovered to be linked to several high-profile crimes in Eastern Europe.

According to Mulgravia News, a documentary about the country is in production by MTV (Mulgravia National Television). The documentary is scheduled for release in the Fall of 2018

Culture and Cuisine

Every February 28, Mulgravia Day, the townspeople of *Katyagrad*, the capital city, gather in the town square to burn in effigy Gustaf Mulgra and his wife Katerina, the country's tyrannical founders, and to partake of *Mulgrafitch*, a fragrant stuffed pastry ("fitch" being the vulgar Mulgravian term for the posterior). Prince Stephan, the current heir to the throne is by all accounts a genial fellow. He can usually be found in one of the many taverns on *Gustafstrasse* (Katyagrad's main thoroughfare) though to the chagrin of the national brewers he is reported to favor imported beer, having a particular weakness for Newcastle Brown.

The national delicacy is *Skutzkwurst,* a spicy sausage made from the entrails of the *Skutzk*, a small arboreal rodent native to the region. The Skutzk appears on the national flag and serves as the official mascot of the national sports teams (see *Sports*, below).

The Mulgravian punk band *Taxi Pankake* is very popular on the world stage. At home a more melodic folk music holds sway, as exemplified by the legendary *Carlotta Korinska* (1911 - 1986). [4]

Education

Mulgravia has a strong educational system. The Ministry of Education is traditional in outlook. For example, the use of calculators is prohibited in high schools. Outsiders might find the arithmetic somewhat daunting as Mulgravia uses a septagesimal (17-based) number system. The origin of the number system is unknown, though a popular legend holds that the principality was settled by a race of giants with eight fingers on each hand, the males of which also used another appendage in their counting.

Mulgravia's leading seat of higher education, the renowned MIT, has rigorous admission standards. Areas of strength include Foreign Affairs and Seal Husbandry.

Currency

The Mulgravian mint issues three coins, the *Pek,* the *Sard,* and the *Mulgravian Crown,* the last valued at approximately 1.5 U.S. dollars. There are 10 Pek to a Sard, and 20 Sard to a Crown. There is an ongoing push towards septagesimalization, which, in spite of opposition by the Mulgravia Board of Accountants, seems likely to be adopted in the near future.

Titles of Nobility

Mulgravia sells titles of nobility including Duke, Baron, and Viscount. Earldoms have recently become available.

Sports

On the second Saturday in May a footrace is held around the perimeter of the country, a distance of approximately 13.5 miles. The race is tremendously popular, sometimes attracting as many as 200 entrants and is covered live on Mulgravia TV Channel 4. The winner receives a purse of 578 Crowns and a bust of Orlov Kinski, Mulgravia's most distinguished long-distance runner, who placed fifth in the Olympic marathon of 1924. Purse and bust are presented in a ceremony held in the gardens of the Royal Palace on the day following the race.

A number of amateur athletes represent Mulgravia in sporting events, most notably unconventional events such as the egg throwing world championship, which Mulgravia hosted and won in 2007.

The Mulgravian people are fanatical about soccer and have a national team that occasionally competes on the world stage. The team's proudest moment came in a world cup qualifying match in 1965 when the *Mulgravia Skutzkhin* (Squirrels) held the mighty England team to a 3-0 victory at Wembley stadium. A week after the game the captain of the Mulgravia team, *Lev Bronsky,* received a letter from the great Bobby Charlton who scored two of the goals in the Wembley encounter. Charlton praised the "gritty determination of the Mulgravia team" and in particular, Bronsky's defensive skills. The Charlton letter, beautifully captioned and framed, held pride of place above the Bronsky mantelpiece for forty-five years until Lev's widow passed away in 2006. It now makes the rounds of the households of the four surviving Bronsky children and will be donated to the National Museum upon their deaths.

Outreach

In recent years, Mulgravia has sought to create an international presence. The National Bureau of Entertainments is currently auditioning talent for the principality's first entry into the Eurovision Song Contest.

References

1. "A Census of Population, Households and Dwellings in Mulgravia 2005". Monstat. Retrieved 3 May 2005.

2. Mulgravia, Myth or Fact?" World Almanac 1929.

3. Justin Madison (1973). *Mulgravia's Ark*. Grobner Books.

4. Temple Downs (1954). *The Divine Lotte: Mulgravia Songbird.* Dark Horse Press.

Rebekka

Donnie K. She recognizes him the instant he turns around but for some reason he doesn't seem to know her. They are in a convenience store and it must be night because it's dark outside. He is standing in line in front of her.

Her first reaction is panic and she wants to run. The merest hint, a grimace or a smirk, is all it would take. Yet there is *nothing*. All he does is smile sweetly at her as he puts a pack of cigarettes and a package of gum on the counter. John Boy in leathers.

Somehow, she finds it within herself to meet his gaze with indifference. She knows him so well, the way a person knows a gangrenous limb. His phone number. His parents' fancy residence on Park Street. The Business classes he is taking at Templeton. Those pretentious holes in the knees of his pants. Their little foray out into the country in his green Mercedes the night of that stupid shindig not another freaking soul in miles her abiding arrogance feeding him with herself enabling his greed. His hands on her, tearing, twisting. The stink of his whisky breath. Then he is inside her. She can feel herself breaking...

He pays for his stuff and heads for the door. But before he leaves, he takes the time to preen in front of the security camera and adjust himself.

Will he be waiting for her outside? It hardly seems to matter.

Then he is behind the register and she is standing alongside him. She fixes him good and steady, square in the eyes. *Hi, I'm Danielle. I'll be bagging for you tonight*, she says as she reaches for something behind her back.

The Assistant II

He didn't need an assistant, but they sent him one anyway. She arrived unannounced one Wednesday morning. A tightly wrapped woman, all bustle and business. She quickly established herself at the spare desk in the corner of his office.

The woman looked familiar. He studied her from time to time as she worked at the desk, trying to figure out when and where they might have met before. He grew up in a small town in South Carolina and she assured him that she had spent her entire life out West. Perhaps she reminded him of somebody that he'd seen on TV, or a writer on the cover of a novel that he'd read? Nothing quite seemed to fit. He finally decided that she looked like a girl he had known in college and resolved to forget about the matter.

She *felt* rather than saw his eyes, crawling over her body like spiders. Always when her own eyes were otherwise occupied and he no doubt thought that she couldn't see him watching her. She assumed at first that it was something about the way she was dressing, and she chose her outfits rather carefully for a few days until she caught herself and dismissed the notion as poppycock

Nonetheless, when he looked at her with those arachnid eyes, it felt as though she was being stripped naked. She found herself looking down at herself every so often to be sure that her blouse was properly buttoned or reaching to adjust her bra, something she would not normally do except in private.

The assistant had the strangest mannerisms. The way she would glance furtively in his direction as though to be sure she had his attention, then reach into her shirt and—he wasn't imagining this—*touch* herself! He was no voyeur and it made him uncomfortable. He remembered seeing a TV show once about a certain type of primate, where the female of the species did something of the sort in order to attract a mate. *Acting out*, they called it. Strangely, it took a while for the significance of this to register.

How to deal with the situation? Her first instinct was to quit right then and there. Then she decided that this was silly. Let herself be driven away by this man before she'd even got started at Ashe & Turner? *Not this tine,* she told herself. She needed this job too badly.

There were several other options, none of them great. She could, of course, just ignore it and go on with her work. Only, she knew enough about men like this to know that this approach was unlikely to fix the problem and might even be seen as a sign of compliance, thereby encouraging him to escalate his behavior. She could go the opposite route and confront him, but she hesitated to make a scene given the tenuous nature of her position here. The employment manual they had given her offered some very specific advice regarding this sort of thing. She could only imagine how this would pan out. He'd deny it and which one they were going to believe, the senior clerk or the assistant? A woman with her background.

In any case, as she admitted to herself in one of her clearer moments, she wasn't sure that what was happening here quite fit the bill. After all, the abuse, thus far at least, was firmly in the realm of the ocular. Was there such a thing as *visual* harassment? In the end, she decided that she would respond in kind. Shame him into retreat.

The way she had of looking at him! As though he'd suddenly up and spouted a second head. He wanted to ask her if there was a problem, but the way she was acting he didn't dare.

***

After a while she found herself responding to his attentions in a way that confused her. Somehow, the office dynamic, a combination of authority and unstated menace—for by now she thought she knew precisely the type of scenarios that would be playing out behind the oh-so-mild manner, the dorky frames—served to provoke something raw in her. Make her want to do with him things that she would have sworn she was done with long ago.

Other times, he came across as needy and sad and all she felt for him was contempt. Then the roles seemed to reverse and suddenly she was the one calling the shots.

"Could you stay for a while tonight? I could use some help."

"I'll bet you could! And what exactly is it that you would want me to do for you?"

There are a couple of things, as it happens. Afterwards we could have dinner, perhaps? There's a lovely little French restaurant just a few blocks... Of course, if you have plans for the evening..."

"Actually, yes."

"Yes you can stay or yes you have plans?"

"No plans. All the same, sugar plum, it's not going to happen."

Sugar plum. Was it a jibe at his manhood? The next day she barely even acknowledged him, as though he had done something to offend her.

By turns surly and sassy, forward and aloof, hot and cold, round and round they went.

One day she volunteered, quite out of the blue, that she once had a twin sister. Her name was *Joy* and she was wonderful.

Once had?

"She ki... she died when we were young."

He was sorry. He would like to have a sister. He didn't have any siblings.

It doesn't matter, she said. *Sometimes I think she is still with me and all the other people in the world are ghosts. Or that it is we who are the ghosts.*

He thought it was beautiful, poetic. A few days later when, in an attempt to draw her out, he asked her to tell him a little more about the sister, she acted surprised, denied ever having said that she had one. He thought he was going crazy. Then she admitted that it was something she had made up and that she too was an only child.

Why would she do that?

Just a bit of fun, a little game she liked to play at times. She smiled at him and he felt like a fool.

And so it went, on and on.

Eventually, he put two and two together and concluded that all this was her way of coming on to him! The touching. The staring. The teasing. It was the only thing that made sense.

He had been alone so long the idea was stimulating. He lay awake at night thinking about it, concocting midnight scenarios. He hardly knew how to respond. One thing was clear. She obviously wanted for him to notice her breasts for she had gone out of her way to make a thing of them, and by now he was willing to do just about anything to please her.

Her strategy had evidently backfired, for now the man was ogling her *openly*. Apparently, he was shameless.

Again she was at sea, and by this time any ideas of harassment claims had taken themselves off the table. Somewhere along the way, the boundary between them had shifted. When she thought about this, she felt like a traitor.

He started to wonder about this strange creature that had invaded his personal space and turned it upside down. How she had shown up so unexpectedly. How he had taken her in so readily. *Perhaps she's a corporate spy*, he thought jokingly.

He decided to make some discreet inquiries. It turned out that none of his colleagues knew anything about her. She was unlisted in the company directory. He played her little game for a while where he pretended to himself that she really was a ghost.

A visit to Personnel. Her file was protected, the level of confidentiality reserved for employees that came to the company via the back door.

Something about the imaginary twin caught in his mind and he churned it over and over. He thought about his youth. About his time at Bedford High and an incident that had happened in his final year there. And then he knew.

***

There was a young girl seventeen years of age and she loved to sing and dance. The girl's name was Rebekka, not Joy, and she did have a sister, though the two were not twins.

One night in the summer of 1997, the girl was beaten and raped by her prom date, a senior at a nearby college. The guy was the son of a prominent businessman who wielded a great deal of influence in town.

Charges were brought. The girl and her family were treated with the utmost civility by the authorities. More civility than people like them were used to and more than they could stand at times. Absence of consent can be a difficult thing to prove in cases where the accused is a boyfriend, they were told. The injuries would of course be a factor, but his… unfortunate history with women was not admissible as evidence.

It didn't seem fair to them? Maybe not, but it was the way the court system worked. The fact that they had only dated a couple of times would not matter and in any case, juries tend to look unfavorably on young girls who carry on relationships with older men.

Trials of this type can be hard on the accuser and the poor girl had already suffered so much. Did they really want to subject her to that?

Perhaps they would prefer to settle out of court. The family of the boy had come through with a rather generous offer, enough to take care of the young lady's immediate medical bills and a whole lot more besides.

The family of the girl declined the offer.

While condemning the egregious behavior, the judge was of the opinion that the defendant had been sufficiently punished with jail time already served. The defendant was a student at a fine college, with a promising career ahead of him. Furthermore, he had expressed genuine remorse for the pain he had caused. What was to be gained, the judge counseled the jury, by ruining another life?

The girl was awarded $5,000 in damages and the guy handed a suspended sentence and remanded to a program of counseling.

Six months after the trial, the girl slashed her wrists. The guy was out whooping it up with his frat boys at the time, boozing and bragging and contemplating future adventures.

But the sister enacted her own form of justice. Picked him up in a bar one night and lured him to a motel room. Slipped something into his drink and took a knife to his belly.

It was twenty years ago and they had barely known each other then. But it was all over the school and in the local newspapers and on TV, and something like that tends to linger on in the mind.

***

Things were better between them now. She was more real with him, less bitter. Less weird. At least it would be that way for a while. Then he would say something dumb that set her off and suddenly they were back to square one. Two wounded animals clawing at each other.

He finally decided that this tension between them would have to be resolved. They would hash it out. He'd explain how he felt about her, that he wanted to take their relationship beyond the workplace. What he knew about her past would, of course, remain hidden for now.

He'd do it this week. Perhaps tomorrow even, if he could only summon up the nerve. He rehearsed the speech in his head, over and over. *We've worked together now for...*

It sounded so lame, she would probably laugh in his face.

She felt more in control that night. Able to assess the situation dispassionately, or so she thought. How strange it was, the way this thing had turned itself so completely on its head. For by now it was clear that if she wanted it to happen between them, then *she* would need to be the one to move things along.

The problem was, she was not much of a mover these days. She had assumed all along that she could have him for the asking, suddenly she was not so sure. After all, she had been wrong about so much else about him. *Little Miss Priss, Clerical Assistant*, she thought sickly, finally wanting something from a man. She laughed uproariously at this. Then she cried. She'd gone off her meds and was at the front end of a downward spiral.

She made all sorts of plans for the two of them, imagined the type of corny couple they would be. Her Rolling Stones and his Mozart. Hiking on the trails in summer, skiing trips to the mountains in winter when they could afford it. Friends over for Thanksgiving dinner. A kitty or two, provided he was not allergic. Squabbling over the funny pages on a Sunday morning. His tea and her coffee. Bitchy before she gets it. Time out from one of their silly old movies for a wham-bam in the middle of the afternoon. She wants him for his body. He wants her for her mind. Her *sweetness*. Those pictures in her head, her lifelong companions.

Did I ever tell you, honey, about the time I…

A doctor's appointment the next day kept him out of the office until noon. By the time he arrived, she was gone. He assumed she was out sick and waited for a call, but the clock ticked on and on and none came.

Then he noticed the unusually tidy desk. Found the note, or rather the pathetic beginnings of one, crumpled up in the wastebasket. No reason. No forwarding address. *Nothing.*

He looked for her everywhere. In supermarkets, gas stations, coffee shops and bars. Conducted Internet searches. Placed ads in personal columns. Posted flyers in public places: HAVE YOU SEEN THIS WOMAN? Even offered a reward, as though she were an outlaw or a lost puppy.

A couple of dead ends, then zilch. He beat his head against the wall in an agony of rage. He felt like a man drowning in his own juices.

Sitting alone on a park bench on a Sunday afternoon with the shrieks of children playing nearby, she thinks again about the man. Wonders how it all might be different now if she'd been just a little… stronger? Braver? Perhaps just a better liar? At the clinic, they warned of the danger of making life-changing decisions while emotionally vulnerable, acting impulsively. Was she still impulsive? Someday, she tells herself, I'll go back and find him. Explain why I cut and ran.

The poor man would wet his pants. Would he hate her, think her a monster? Or just a lunatic?

It had been so long. Would he even care?

Jake and the Rat

Jake walks into the hall and comes across a staircase that he had not noticed before. The staircase leads to a suite of lavishly furnished rooms. The old house is grander than he had known...

One of the rooms contains a row of beds, all made up. Like a ward of hospital beds awaiting accident victims on a Saturday night.

Who are they for?

Another room appears to be a study. There is an old oak desk littered with expired claims checks and unanswered letters, a lamp and a swivel chair. Bookshelves filled with books, except that the spines on the books have no names on them. Faces dance in picture frames. Jake sees a girl he knew once in one. The girl committed suicide when she was just twenty-five years old, following a liaison with a deadbeat from the mill.

A group of people are gathered on a laundry room across the hall. Sigmund Freud, the foreman at the mill, the Marquis de Sade, Linda from Human Resources, a major league pitcher from Paraguay – Jesus something or other, and the kid from *Leave it to Beaver*. Last month the foreman fired Jake, something to do with lack of commitment. Now he has the nerve to invite himself to his home! The whole charade smacks of the game of Clue and while the-foreman-in-the-office-with-a-pink-slip might seem the obvious choice, Jake has a better idea.

A fancy bathroom with a giant portrait of Quasimodo on the wall facing the commode. Jake takes advantage of the opportunity to relieve himself. When he gets out his father is standing there. This is strange because the man died ten years ago.

How's it hangin', sport? Jake's father says.

Jake looks down and checks himself, then snatches up a loose-leaf binder from the shelf over the sink and waves it in the air.

Lookee here, it's done! Stayed up all night to finish it.

How's that for commitment, his father shouts through a hole in the wall. *Half his life and the bum leaves it to the last freaking day*!

This is one f-word that Jake has never heard the old man use before.

It's a family show, explains the Beaver.

Fuck that, says Jesus.

And the pig he rode in on, growls the Marquis.

Works for me, says Freud.

Linda checks her watch. *Time to go, pumpkin*, she says as she bends over to button Jake's coat and kiss him goodbye. Freud and the Marquis exchange a wry grin as she heads off to commune with Quasimodo.

Jake is presenting his report to the class, on "The role of recombinant DNA in the development of the mushroom." There is a new teacher standing at the back of the room. The teacher looks suspiciously like Jake's father, except that he has long hair like Jesus that completely covers his face. His classmates are all cheering and Jake feels very proud. But behind the hair, the teacher is mad.

The teacher reaches into his pants and pulls out a switch. He then accuses Jake of lying, though, in fact, Jake has never lied but once or twice in his entire life. Once to a girl who turned up on a slab with a belly full of Drano and once about his name. Turns out Jake's real name is Bryan and Bryan has a pet rat named Percy that Jake keeps hidden in a box underneath the stairs and brings out when things get rough.

On your bike, bitch, says the teacher after the whipping but Jake's butt is too sore to even consider it. Besides, he never even owned a bike, though he does happen to know some boys on the East Side who could fix him up with one on the fly.

See, now this here is what I'm talking about, says the teacher to the class. *He's a BUM. Always was and always–*

ALL I EVER WANTED WAS FOR YOU TO LOVE ME, Jake screams at his tormentor, but the message goes unheard because Jake's features are even now starting to form into the shape of the girl he once knew and it is himself that he is addressing.

It feels as though Jake has been gone an eternity, though in reality it may have been only an instant. When he finally arrives home, all bloodied and bruised, everybody has left apart from Freud and the Marquis, and the two of them are on the phone with Tony Soprano arranging for a pick-up of wet goods.

Seeking a different form of closure, Jake calls up a psychic help line and speaks with a woman named Wanda. Wanda tells Jake that his name is not really Jake, who does he think he's kidding, she's a psychic and if he can only get all these people out of his head then one day he will be elected Minister for Foreign Affairs and he will appoint a *rat* for his Deputy.

Jake says he hopes this call is not costing anything because she's full of it, and Wanda assures him that all 1-900 numbers are free of charge.

After they get off the phone with the psychic, Percy tells Jake to look in the trunk under the stairs.

Jake opens up the trunk and inside he finds a box full of dreams.

Boxes

"... they live in boxes, you know."

A snippet of conversation that I overhear from the other side of the table. My daughter-in-law is speaking to my son during a family get-together. We're eating dinner at an Italian restaurant.

"We all live in boxes," I say.

They look at me questioningly.

"Big boxes, small boxes, black and white and yellow and red boxes. My box. Your box. Boxes that shut out the light and separate us from each other. The boxes that society builds for us. Most of all, the boxes we build for ourselves."

"That's true," she says, "but these are real boxes. They live in them below the overpass at 75 and Main."

"*Oh*, I say."

Purple Dress

One spoon of instant and two spoons of sugar in the Disney mug with the broken handle. The best way to start your day. Itchy scalp and bog mouth. Funky smelling garbage sticky beer slops broken things. The purple dress lying crumpled up on the floor like a corpse.

Bags and rags everywhere. Her things. The makeup case with the busted mirror. Granny undies and a pair of bright red tube socks. The I Ching and the Kabbala. A stack of romance books and one about a new type of meditation.

She'll be back for it all sometime this afternoon.

Will you be here then?

Dump the old newspapers down on the floor flop down on the couch snatch up the remote. One click and there. Reruns of Bonanza—costume jewelry half price for the next 150 callers—soap operas—talk shows with slutty housewives. The Weather Channel. Weather girl Jane sunny and bright.

Depression moving in. Calm now but severe storms with flash floods expected later in the day. All hell in the offing.

***

Back in the kitchen, her plates and bowls ambush you. Call you a dick and ask what you will do when they're gone. Moldy cheese and sour milk in the fridge. And the happy pills are almost out. The carving knife on the counter top is winking at you in the sunlight. *Beckoning,* like a clean male lover.

BUBBLING AND POPPING. Pour it in and there you go. Folger's in your cup.

Icky combo of coffee and pills makes you gag but you keep it down. Necessity is the mother— the last two.

Soon it all seems vaguely funny.

***

Met her in a hostel in a bad part of LA one Tuesday afternoon years ago. Pleasantly plump and paranoid. You remember like it was yesterday, the contours of every blemish, every last sore. The lines of demarcation between pleasure and pain.

Said *Waddup* or words to that effect. She told you not to address her, she doesn't speak to strange men in places like this. Like was scared you were some sort of homicidal conversationalist.

Does she speak to strange women, then? Not that there's anything wrong with that.

You're a queer one, she said.

Helped her out in a fracas outside some thirty minutes later. Bought her a hot meal.

When you got back to the hostel the place was deserted. She told you she's the type of girl who likes to pay her debts and if you put on a raincoat she would bend over. You said it wasn't necessary, but if that's what she wanted then you would prefer a more intimate style.

Afterwards she spoke a LOT. Wondered what you'd got yourself into. Her real name is Gwendolyn though people all call her Wendy. Restless curious type, likes to live life on the edge. Gets around the country on busses, bums rides whenever she can. Has been out of circulation for a while (??). Recently Jewish. Daddy trades futures, mommy drinks and doesn't have one. Hasn't seen either one of them in ten years. Serially monogamous equal opportunity lover (likes men and women, one at a time). *Loves* animals. Gave birth once. Used to be an Egyptian princess. Menopausal monster. Has a Native American spirit guide named *Greywolf* that watches out for her.

***

You remember things she said when she was happy, when she was sad.

She'll wear you like a coat. Eat you alive if you let her, chew up your heart and stomp on your bones. Such silly sounding words. Playing Goth, you assumed. When you asked why, she shrugged and said "It has a tendency to happen" with the people in her life.

Getting wasted together on the road back from the Grand Canyon in the old Buick you fixed up. The birthplace of humanity, no less.

One fucked up hole, you observed in typical fashion.

She must have misconstrued your entendre. *Not all of it,* she said in a strange, quiet voice. *There is so much beauty in the world, only we cover it up with our hatred and our lies. People and places. Colors so bright it will make you cry. Stay with me and I'll show you.*

Whether crazy bitch or sage, you never could quite decide. Nonetheless, you replay this over and over in your head. It feels like probing an exposed nerve with your tongue.

Huddling together on a park bench on a frigid day in January that was all black and white. The two of you had just been thrown out of your apartment and had no place else to go. Pitching snowballs at each other. She called you a wuss. Pitching home truths following a dust-up in June. You had a better throwing arm that day.

Holding you nights when you had the shakes.

Told her once following a rage of passion she has the greenest eyes ever. She got them from the princess, she said, and you and she are kindred spirits. Soul mates. Her BFF where the first F stands for *friend.*

Now she has wild unprotected cybersex with balding virtual husband boris8u. Writes poetry to herself in the dead of night that she burns in the light of day. Whispers nothings to no one. Maintains a website devoted to the inner lives of past creatures Mr. Chuckles and Dreamboat that she updates once every two weeks. Goes wherever she chooses, does whoever she wants.

Throws out what she no longer needs.

You pick the dress up off the floor, fold it neatly over a chair. Survey the landscape one last time before returning to the kitchen. She told you once that the two of you knew each other in a past life, that she'll look for you in the next. Perhaps she'll find you there.

Two for the Show

Female Game Show Contestants

Dear Professor Smithies,

I am a health care professional living in East Los Angeles. I am writing in regard to your recent article in Psychology Now. I would like to congratulate you on the article. One cannot help but be impressed by your insight into this important, and thus far overlooked, aspect of human behavior. The field of behavioral psychology has been greatly enriched by your work...

***

My name is Frank Smithies and I love to watch TV game shows. Always have. The long running game show *Hedge Your Bets* is a nightly ritual in my household. My wife and I have watched the show just about every night of our married life and we've been married 25 years! I swear there are times when even the family pets seem to be paying attention.

HYB is set up similarly to the popular game show *Jeopardy,* though the questions tend to be more uptown—less De Caprio and more Da Vinci, if you catch my drift.

Three contestants compete against each other in answering general knowledge questions with differing dollar amounts and there is a final round, where the players can risk any or all of their accumulated stash on a single question. They all get to keep the cash they earn and the winner comes back to play again the next day.

Over the years, I have observed a strange phenomenon. When a man is in the lead going into the final round, he invariably wagers enough to win the game. *Not so women.* Often times it happens that a woman, especially when competing against two men, will wager low and end up losing, even though she may have been ahead throughout the game and answered the final question correctly. If the monetary amounts involved were substantial then this approach might make sense, but a few thousand bucks? — *come on!*

An armchair psychologist will no doubt explain this behavior with catchalls such as "women are by nature less competitive," or "women tend to err on the side of caution," but I must to point out that it happened last week with a female professional poker player and once with a woman who claimed she enjoys skydiving and bungee jumping!

I cite a recent show as a case in point. Contestants Chuck, an attorney and the returning champ, Ramona, a waitress, and some clown by the name of Todd. (I forget what it was they said Todd did for a living but he was never in the game anyway, so who cares.) Dollar amounts going into the final round as follows:

Chuck $4500
Ramona $7200
Todd $750

You can probably guess what's coming next. Chuck wagered every last dime and Ramona zip. The final question was easy. They all knew it, even the hapless Todd, and Chuck doubled his money and got to come back.

As for Ramona, I thought to myself, smart but not *too* smart and somewhat to the annoyance of my wife, who, it must be said, is a little challenged in the humor department, I could not resist trotting out a few of my old chestnuts: *That's why we'll never see a woman president in this country, hope she invests it wisely*, and my all-time favorite, *if she only had a pair, she'd be a man*!

As you will have no doubt gathered, I am something of a student of human nature and you're perhaps thinking, *there goes another armchair psychologist.* In point of fact, nothing could be further from the truth. It so happens you are in the company of none other than the Assistant Dean of Humanities at the renowned Templeton

College in South Carolina, and I might add, one of the world's leading authorities in the area of psychology of gaming. Why, just last month, I published an article on this very subject in the well-known monthly *Psychology Now,* linking the aforementioned pathology to the Electra Complex. The article was titled, "The Ramona Syndrome" and if I am not mistaken, has already garnered some small notoriety within the discipline.

***

PS: I would like to bring to your attention a certain item. Please find enclosed a press clipping concerning a young woman from my neighborhood. I will not comment on the clipping as it speaks for itself, but I am sure you will find it of interest.

The press clipping, which I had not noticed before, fell out when I shook the envelope.

> During the show, Ramona told the audience that she is twenty-four years of age and has a six-year-old daughter. She was more candid about her life with this reporter. "I am a single mother with no child support. I work at a local diner and bring home around $1200 a month with tips and overtime. The monthly rent on our one-bedroom condo runs $625 and the landlord is threatening to raise it again...

Efficiency, this is the key to successful college administration. This and a good no-nonsense attitude. I didn't take the time to look at the clipping, which promptly found its way into the trash. As for the letter, I had my secretary scan it for my files.

Consolation Prize

Daniel Santos started, a little embarrassed as his daughter Linda entered the room.

"Why are you watching this old tape again, poppy, it's so *boring*. Anyway, you *lost*!"

Daniel looked up at his daughter and beamed. His pride and joy, all he had left in the world since he'd lost his wife Juanita to breast cancer five years ago. Time passed by so quickly, he couldn't believe that Linda was now twelve years old.

"Don't fuss, chica, it's almost over."

The tape was one of those old Betamax affairs, the type that went out of use years ago. Daniel had viewed this recording so many times, it was a wonder the tape wasn't worn out. The format of the show had changed a little in the thirteen years since Daniel was on it. At that time only the winner kept the cash they earned, while the two runners-up had to settle for a cheap consolation prize.

***

"First we come to our returning champion Eric, who was up against two very good players today. His response?"

SWEDEN

Sorry, Sweden is incorrect. How much will it cost him?

$3,000. That will drop him down to $2100. Over to John.

FINLAND

Finland is the correct answer. And his wager?

Hello—everything! That doubles his score to $12,800. Now over to Daniel, who was leading with $9,000. Did he come up with Finland?"

FINLAND

"Yes he did! Did he wager enough?"

"$3,000. That brings his total to $12,000. He'll finish in second place, and guess what John, you're our new champion!"

A few groans of frustration from the studio audience mixed in with the applause. Daniel looked out over the audience, fuming. He'd miscalculated. Had he wagered more wisely, he would have wound up with eighteen thousand dollars and won the game.

Eighteen grand! A fortune to people like them. He hadn't been able to concentrate, though, his mind was elsewhere. He and Juanita had been trying for two years to conceive. Seemed that these days it was all he could think about—even at a time like this. Neither of them was young and there was only so much time…

"We'll see John again tomorrow. Second and third place contestants will receive a precious gift from our sponsor, Shane's Underwear. A year's supply of boxers."

Had the man said *precious?* He must have misheard. It was probably generous, though even that was a stretch. *Boxers*, for God's sake! He didn't even wear the things, preferring the warmth of the tight-fitting kind.

Then he remembered a silly article Juanita had shown him last week in one of her women's magazines. Who knows, maybe the boxers would help.

The Streetwalker

When Jerry was twelve, he accompanied his mother on a weeklong trip to France. Jerry's father was scheduled to go with them, but something important came up at the last minute and he was forced to cancel. Jerry's father was a senior partner for one of the more prestigious law firms in the city. The man worked long hours and since Jerry did not have many friends, he and his mother spent a lot of time in each other's company.

They stayed in Paris, in a small hotel three blocks from the Champs-Élysées. Jerry's mother signed the register *Mrs. Vanessa Polk*, though her actual given name was Vera, *and son Jerrold,* though nobody ever called him that.

The hotel was unlike any Jerry had seen before—tall and thin like his mother. It looked fancy on the outside but was quite shabby inside, with small dusty rooms with cheap prints on the walls, and a tiny elevator about the size of those phone booths that disappeared with the advent of cell phones.

Jerry's mother was in the habit of taking regular walks back in New York for the sake of her figure, so the two of them spent a good part of every day in Paris traipsing from one art gallery or museum to another. When returning to their hotel one evening, they took a wrong turn and ended up on a street with once grand three-story houses, now gone to seed. There was a line of heavily made up women standing on the street, spaced at intervals of twenty feet or so apart. Jerry asked his mother if the women were all waiting for somebody. His mother's face turned pink and she told him not to look at them.

As they reached the end of the street, Jerry glanced back and happened to catch the eye of one of the women. She was red-haired and pretty, and she looked very young, perhaps only a few years older than Jerry himself.

The girl wore her hair piled on top of her head in a bun, and Jerry noticed that she sported an unusual feature that either detracted from or enhanced her appearance, he couldn't say which—an oval shaped birthmark near the hairline on the right side of her forehead.

The girl smiled at Jerry in a lopsided sort of way and shrugged, as if to say, *I don't know what I'm doing here either.*

***

Thirty-nine years to the day had passed since the encounter with the girl on the street in Paris. The likeness of the girl was indelibly carved into the architecture of Jerry's brain; axons, neurons, and synapses configured to the precise contours of body, face, most of all, that enigmatic smile. He had always wondered about this, her effect on him.

Jerry was sitting in an armchair, sipping on a fine *Pinot Noir* that he'd bought to mark the occasion. He picked up the photograph that he'd removed earlier in the day from the wall safe in the cellar. As always, his stomach began to churn as he looked at it.

The photo had come to Jerry's attention with the death of his mother five years ago. It might have been forever consigned to obscurity but for the refined tastes of a relative. Jerry was disposing of his mother's things as a way of keeping himself together. There was a collection of romance novels. Jerry had offered the novels to his cousin, who he thought would like them, only to be told that she doesn't "read such trash." The photo fell out of a book named *Charlotte's Viking* as he was packing up the novels to ship to Goodwill.

The photo was a close-up of Jerry's mother as a young woman. A drab monochrome affair, probably snapped with one of those old box cameras that were in use at the time. Written on the back were the place and the date, *Coney Island, July 25, 1947.* The girl who, eight years later, was destined to become Jerry's mother would have been sixteen years old then. She was smiling sassily into the camera, the way young people are wont to do, pulling her hair back from her face and pointing to something on her forehead. Jerry couldn't be sure since the photo was badly faded, but it looked like an oval moon, identical in location to the one on the girl inside his head.

There was an unmistakable resemblance between the girl in the picture and the young streetwalker in Paris. Round face, dimpled cheeks, the way the left side of the mouth curled upwards a little more than the right when she smiled, lending a touch of roguishness to the face. You might have thought the two were twins, though the age difference suggested a slightly different scenario.

Jerry's mother hailed from a working-class family from the east side of Boston. Jerry had never met any of them, ties with that side of the family having been well and truly severed before he was born, but he had researched a little of the family history. His maternal grandparents, Frank and Margaret Byrne, had emigrated from Ireland between the two World Wars, a few years prior to his mother's birth. As far as Jerry was aware, there were no relatives in France and of course he knew nothing about the girl. But the paternal family grapevine held that his mother had been "a bit of a lass" prior to her marriage, and one of the uncles was kind enough to pass on something he'd learned somehow, concerning "a hasty departure to Europe in her early twenties following an alarming expansion in the midriff region."

It couldn't all be coincidence. Looking at this picture, Jerry wondered if he had ever really known his mother.

The room was starting to grow dark with the setting sun. Jerry switched on a lamp and poured himself another glass of wine. This time of day was always the hardest to deal with now, the gray period between the time the markets closed on the West Coast and the night set in with its shroud of anonymity. The time of elephant men like himself, and goblin women.

Jerry took stock of his life. No romantic partner, no siblings, a few professional acquaintances—none that he would call friends. He pulled the letter out of his wallet and examined it for the umpteenth time.

Picard et Associés
Détectives, efficace et discret
127 rue Saint-Martin
72001 Paris, France
29 avril 2005

Dear Monsieur, we thank you for your enquiry…

Efficace et discret. Would they be able to find her, as the tone of this letter implied? The very idea was fantastic.

Then again, what if they did? Jerry had led a sheltered life, but he knew enough about the ways of the world to know that things rarely turned out well for women who sold themselves. Jerry was, by nature, a generous man—the type of generosity that wrote yearly checks to organizations with names like *World Outreach*, *The New England Psychiatric Foundation*, *Battered Wives of America.* How would it feel to look into the face of poverty? Sickness? Misery and pain? Madness, even? Assuming she was even still alive. And what was there to say? *I saw you once on the street, Madame. You were young and pretty then.*

It was time to start thinking about dinner, though Jerry was barely hungry. There was a steak in the freezer that he could defrost. *Perhaps I'll fry up a potato in honor of the occasion*, he thought with a wry smile. Fact was, he never ate anything fried these days. Not since his doctor had found a cholesterol problem. Better safe than sorry. *They'll inscribe that on my tombstone*, he thought bitterly.

Jerry crumpled up the letter and tossed it into the wastebasket. He cast a final glance at the photo and placed it in an envelope. At midnight, he'd take the photo back down to the cellar and lock it in the safe, where it would remain untouched until this time next year. Next year would be the fortieth. Perhaps he'd treat himself to a bottle of Dom Perign—

Suddenly, Jerry was finding it hard to catch his breath. He fell back in the chair as a sharp pain seized his chest and poured down his left arm. *Was he having a heart attack*?

The room had become very bright. The two women were standing there. Both looked exactly as he remembered them that day on the street in Paris, his mother tall and proud, the girl bemused. His mother was pointedly ignoring him, pulling back the girl's hair and tenderly stroking the birthmark.

See how beautiful, she murmured to nobody in particular.

But the girl wasn't looking at Jerry's mother. She was pointing at Jerry, as though she intended to help him, or at least draw attention to his plight. Instead, she smiled that mischievous smile. His mother's smile.

Look what you raised, she said.

Jerry would not be treated this way in his own home by a dead woman and a trollop. He opened his mouth to tell them as much, but all he could do was gasp.

I'M GOING TO DIE, his mind screamed as blackness washed over him...

***

Just after dawn, Jerry opened his eyes. The pain in his chest had abated and the women were gone. Everything looked the same, but if felt as though something in the room had shifted.

After a while, Jerry got up and walked over to the trashcan. He fished out the ball of paper and straightened it out. The latter felt like a lead weight in his hand. A doorway to another world, or a dead end, or the proverbial road to hell.

He sat down at the desk and reached for pen and paper.

Dear Monsieur Picard...

Vanishing Point at the End of the World

You hit the skids and there is no traction. You wonder if there ever was any. *Maybe*, a voice beyond the horizon close to the vanishing point mutters. Cars and houses trees flailing limbs your chemistry teacher from high school a cricket bat your mother and sister the contents of a lunch box a one-time lover friends and foes rushing headlong towards you a mind fuck of a Picasso nightmare with Jackson Pollock highlights. When you crash through the gap it hurts, but not too much, and you sink into some kind of turgid mud. You ought to be scared out of your mind but you're not and it makes you proud, and you have time to wonder if this is wrong. Close by is a couple with a young child and two cats, and a cart pulled by a donkey with ears made of cotton candy. The sky is a vivid shade of pink disappearing to black and the sun is big and bold, like the moon. Out to sea a boat with fire painted on its sails and screamers churning the surface. Somewhere in that mess must be life, you think, and if you only look hard enough you will find it.

Publication Credits

Assistant: *Foliate Oak*, December, 2013.
Assistant II (preliminary version): *Grub Street*, May, 2014.
Birthday Party: *Lotus-eater,* September, 2019.
Boxes: *Ink in Thirds*, February, 2017.
Consolation Prize: *Smokebox*, April, 2014.
Delivery: *Every Writer's Resource*, May, 2018.
Double Take: *Meat for Tea: The Valley Review*, December, 2013.
Einstein's Wardrobe: *The Rusty Nail*, December, 2012.
Female Game Show Contestants: *Journal of Microliterature*, January, 2016.
Fragments: *Rock & Sling*, February, 2014.]
Fruit: *Hirschworth*, October 2013; *Adelaide Magazine Literary Awards Anthology*, June, 2017; *Ink & Sword*, August, 2018.
Jake and the Rat: *Danse Macabre*, September, 2014; *Literally Stories,* July, 2018; *Exterminating Angel*, Spring 2020.
Just the Two of Us: *Literary Orphans*, December, 2019.
Moving On: *Every Writer*, October, 2013; *Calliope*, Spring, 2015.
Mulgravia: *Nazar Look*, December, 2013.
Portrait of a Genius: *Prague Revue,* December, 2013.
Placebo: *Literary Juice*, June/July, 2013.
Purple Dress: *Adelaide Literary Magazine*, December, 2017.
The Streetwalker: *Futures Trading*, January, 2014; *CCLaP Weekender*, August, 2015. First section published in *Flash: The International Short-Short Story Magazine*, October, 2013.
Time Lapse: *Bewildering Stories*, May, 2012 (under pseudonym Arthur Pinte).
Troll Bot: *Calliope*, January 2014; *Every Writer*, August, 2014.
Twins: *Olentangy Review*, September 2014; *Maine Review*, August, 2015.
Vanishing Point at the End of the World: *Postcard Poems and Prose*, April, 2016.

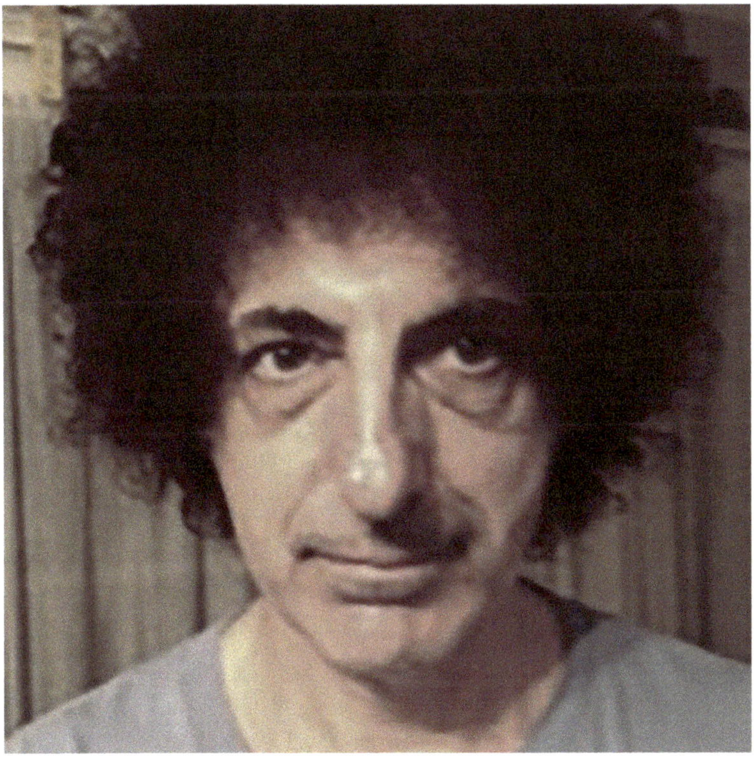

Denis Bell is a maker of both mathematical formulas and small fictions, which he believes, weirdly, that he draws from a common font. He was born and raised in London, England and studied at the Universities of Manchester and Warwick. His scientific work has been recognized by national funding, an Outstanding Scholarship Award from the University of North Florida and a Research Professorship at MSRI in Berkeley, California. Linguistically challenged in earlier life (as evidenced by three attempts to obtain an English O-level!), he started writing fiction relatively recently. His writing has been published in *Grub Street*, *The Maine Review*, *Flash: The International Short-Short Story Magazine*, *Journal of Microliterature*, *Literary Orphans* and many other print and online literary magazines and journals. Most of his ramblings, literary and otherwise can be found at https://www.unf.edu/~dbell.

Louise Freshman Brown is a painter and mixed medium artist whose works have been featured in exhibitions in museums and galleries in the United States and Europe. Solo exhibits include; Piirto Gallery, Helsinki, Finland, Everson Museum, Syracuse, NY, The Museum of Contemporary Art, Jacksonville, Jacksonville, FL, The Deland Museum of Art, DeLand, FL, Monique Goldstrom Gallery, NYC, City Center Theatre, NYC, Albertson-Peterson Gallery, Winter Park, FL, Lufrano Intercultural Gallery, Jacksonville, FL, Hector Gallery, Gainesville, FL, Jacksonville International Airport, Jacksonville, FL

Group exhibitions include Galleria Retro & Arte, Venice, Italy, Advice Konsthall, Sollentuna, Sweden, Jane Haslem Gallery, Washington, DC, Women's Art Cooperative, Van Nuys, CA, The William Whipple Art Gallery, Marshall, MN, New York Academy of Art, NYC, Boca Raton Museum of Art, Boca Raton, FL, Montgomery College, Rockville, MD, The Cummer Museum of Art and Gardens, Jacksonville, FL, Barbara Gillman Gallery, Miami, FL,

Park Plaza Castle, Boston, MA, Childs Gallery, NYC, Linda Hayman Gallery, Boca Raton, FL, Polk Museum, Lakeland, FL, Arts on Douglas, New Smyrna Beach, FL, St. Johns Performing Arts Center, Orange Park, FL, Barbara Gillman Gallery, Miami, FL

Freshman Brown is from Oneida, NY and received her B.F.A. in Painting and M.F.A. in Painting/Printmaking from Syracuse University, Syracuse, NY. She is a Professor Emerita of Art at The University of North Florida, Jacksonville, FL where she has been regularly awarded for excellence in teaching, service and scholarship. In 2005 she received the Outstanding Scholarship Award and in 2007 the Distinguished Professor Award. In 2018 she received the Ann McDonald Baker Art Ventures Award. For the past 40 years, she has conducted workshops and lectures nationally and internationally.

CPSIA information can be obtained
at www.ICGtesting.com
Printed in the USA
BVHW061008051020
590310BV00009B/370

9 781952 411335